CATACOMBS OF TIME

A SWORD AND SORCERY NOVELLA

DYLAN DOOSE

BONUS SHORT STORY INSIDE!

BOOK DESCRIPTION

CATACOMBS OF TIME

"**Dylan Doose is a master.**"—**Amazon reviewer**

It's going to be a long and bloody night.

The clock is ticking and Dr. De'Brouillard has a date. Dinner is at the Graves and a contract to cure one of the cursed is sitting on the plate. But when an old and dear friend reaches out from murky shadow for a helping hand, will the Doctor take it, risking all if he ends up being late?

New heroes join the fray. Are they friend or foe?

Dr. Gaige De'Brouillard believes science, not magic, conquers all. Even death is just an equation to be solved.

Malory "Butcher" Dahmer knows that life is but a dream, no wickedness, no sorcery too strange or obscene.

An Academic and a Gangster make for an interesting team.

Don't miss the dark fantasy that reviewers are calling 'visceral,' 'fantastic,' and 'intriguing'—get your copy of Catacombs of Time today!

This edition includes a FREE Bonus Short Story!

ALSO BY DYLAN DOOSE

SWORD AND SORCERY SERIES:

Fire and Sword (Volume 1)

Catacombs of Time (Volume 2)

I Remember My First Time (A Sword and Sorcery short story; can be read at any point in the series)

The Pyres (Volume 3)

Ice and Stone (Volume 4)

As They Burn (Volume 5)

Black Sun Moon (Volume 6)

Embers on the Wind (Volume 7)

RED HARVEST SERIES:

Crow Mountain (Volume 1)

∽

For info, excerpts, contests and more, join Dylan's Reader Group!

Website: www.DylanDooseAuthor.com

Catacombs of Time Copyright © 2015 by Dylan Doose.

I Remember My First Time Copyright © 2016 by Dylan Doose

All rights reserved.

This book is a work of fiction. All names, characters, locations, and incidents are products of the author's imagination, or have been used fictitiously. Any resemblance to actual persons living or dead, locales, or events is entirely coincidental.

The uploading, scanning, and distribution of this book in any form or by any means—including but not limited to electronic, mechanical, photocopying, recording, or otherwise—without the permission of the copyright holder is illegal and punishable by law. Please purchase only authorized editions of this work, and do not participate in or encourage electronic piracy of copyrighted materials. Your support of the author's rights is appreciated.

CATACOMBS OF TIME
   e-ISBN: 9780994828323
   print ISBN: 9781775235088

www.DylanDooseAuthor.com

CHAPTER ONE

THE WIND OF MEMORY

The moon was red that night. It peeked through the only part of sky not hidden away by the leaden clouds of the manic storm that shifted from bouts of light mist descending from the heavens, to downpours that made it hard to breathe and see. Lightning split the sky, illuminating it momentarily, then leaving it in shadow once more. Thunder resonated, and it was as if the gods themselves were waging war high above with the cannons and arms of the cosmos, and the storm was the fallout of a battle whose combatants were indifferent to the plight of man.

Below the moon and the clouds, where the rain poured down and the lightning threatened destruction, was the University of Villemisère, which had stood in this place for three hundred years, since the time of the first appearance of the Rata Plaga in Brynth. Five stories of lecture halls and laboratories, of studios and dormitories, of mess halls and infirmaries, and long, high-ceilinged corridors with dim lamps dampening the souls of those ambitious youth who braved the years of solitude and anguish that the university promised.

The wind blasted against the front doors. They swung ajar and the draft gusted its way through the vast cylindrical atrium, with its dead gray walls that looked black in the gloom, but for the spaces that had a sleepy orange haze cast by weak lamps. The wind whirled around, an invisible tornado that flew up the wooden stairs, worn by so many years of students and professors hurrying between classes, and then turned left down a corridor, scraping away gray flakes of paint as it went. It put out a lamp nearly a second before it reached its dying place in the library, the smallest breeze now, just a whisper of the thing it had been.

Two forms sat hunched forward over a scarred wooden table. They were alone in the library at this late hour and their conversation was deep, carrying their minds to a different place, and so they cared not for the fury that came down from beyond. They did not notice the wind.

"What you are proposing, Gaige… What it is that you are proposing…" Professor Lumire began, his words reverberating in his swaying, saggy cheeks. "It is not science. It is not medicine." Lumire paused again and lit his long wooden pipe, the light from the match painting shadows above the old doctor's wrinkles as he frowned, deep in thought. "Gaige," he said sternly. "You have just this last year finished your schooling, and already you would reject its teachings?"

Gaige scowled at this remark and swiveled uncomfortably in his chair across from Lumire, wondering if his teacher and mentor knew him at all.

"I reject nothing. I wish only to expand my knowledge, to expand all knowledge." Gaige kept his voice calm, but his heart was pounding. He had waited two full years before revealing his thoughts and research to Lumire, and this was not the reaction he had hoped for.

"Expand knowledge, you say?" Lumire leaned across the table, his eyes so wide Gaige thought they might just pop from the old man's skull. "In... in bloody sorcery?" Lumire whispered the last word, and he turned his head to the doors of the library to make sure no one was there.

"Not sorcery. I am a mortal man. My powers will always be that of a mortal man. How far those powers can go, I am not sure. Science will be the answer." Science was his religion, his faith, his occultism. Science was the hope of mankind. "Science is beyond sorcery. What I will come to learn will not even the battlefield between us and those with arcane blood... it will dominate it," Gaige said, his face hovering close to Lumire's above the library table.

He could see every nuance of his mentor's expression, but Lumire could not see his. Gaige always wore his iron-beaked doctor's mask, for that was the identity he preferred over that of a sickly addict. The mask was the face he showed the world and the veil that hid him from view.

Lumire stared at him and Gaige looked away first, offering his mentor that small token of respect. He sat back and took out his steel pipe, then reached a hand to his beaked mask and tampered with a mechanism, opening a slot in the right side. There he inserted the pipe, then closed the two nostrils with a flick of another very small lever. He drew a match, lit it by running it across the side of the iron beak, put the flame to the bowl, and inhaled. His mask was airtight now, so the moon's widow packed into the pipe burned at a rapid pace. Gaige listened to the shush of the cinders as he took in the smoke. He opened the nostrils of his beak, removed the pipe, and held the smoke deep in his lungs.

He exhaled. The smoke of the moon's widow, a plant so potent that even the inhalation of its ground petals' aroma could produce soothing effects, burst from the mask's nostrils.

Lumire's frown dragged the corners of his mouth lower

and deepened the wrinkles that ran down toward his jaw. "We've discussed this—"

"And we are not discussing it again." Gaige shrugged. "I am sick."

Gaige had always been sick. He was born with a leg that was hardly a twisted strip of bone, with cords of stringy muscle that refused to function on all but the most rudimentary level. It was a weak excuse for a limb. Despite this, Gaige was not weak. He now viewed the agonizing limb as an excellent source for experimentation. Through the study of science and medicine and its applications upon himself, Gaige was fighting, and he was winning against the cruelty of his own design, training the leg to be stronger at a cost of ever-increasing pain. Of course there were other side effects, those of the manner of mental phenomena, those of the physical body, and those of a social nature. They were effects he documented but they did not stop his research.

As to the pain... Pain or not, he refused to cut the leg off. He kept it as a reminder of his humanity.

"The populace will see your science as sorcery," Lumire said. "They will see it as playing God. Worse yet, the seekers will put an end to any research. The lord regent will come down with all his wrath upon the university just for association with your name if you continue in this dreadful dabbling!"

Gaige was shattered by disappointment. He had been wrong to come to Lumire, the one person he thought would understand. "Maybe," he said, keeping his tone even, betraying none of his bitter emotion. "Maybe a time will come where the idea is welcomed."

Lumire slammed his hand down hard on the table; the teacups rattled and the warm liquid sloshed over the sides. "My most favored student, you are at times blinded by your own desire to discover! It pushes you into the direction of black space."

With those words, even Gaige's disappointment snuffed like a dying match, and in its place came the certainty that Lumire had never been the true man of science Gaige had believed him to be. He saw before him now only an old, broken man, bowing to convention. And he had no one to blame but himself, for he had seen something that had never been there. "That is a foolish thing to say, professor. For how can a man ever be blinded by a desire for discovery? A man with such a heart can only ever increase his sight."

"No... It is not our right, not our right as men." The professor bowed his head, sadness crawling into his thoughtful frown.

"I have no expectation of your help. I have no expectation that you will work by my side. Only tell me if you have any books in this great library of yours on the curing of curses." Gaige leaned forward, the tip of his beak almost offensively close to his professor's nose. But Gaige wanted to look into his teacher's eyes; he wanted to see in them the lie when Lumire claimed there were no such books.

Gaige extended his arms and panned them around the library. Floor to ceiling, the walls were covered with tight shelves of books. Dim oil lamps hung from outward poles built into the shelves. To reach the highest shelves, a ladder was needed, and a fall that could kill was risked. It was said to be the world's second largest library. The largest belonged to the Imperial City of Brynth, and it held certain archives allowed entry only to his Holy Majesty.

Lumire lifted his tea, the cup in one hand, the saucer in the other, the two rattling together as he trembled.

Gaige stood and turned around. He was dizzy from the moon's widow, and the shelves around him reached up and up into the unknown darkness.

"What about on the highest shelf back there? Or over in the foreign historical documents? Or the untranslated rune writings from Ygdrasst? All I ask for is your guidance. I came to you like a son to his father. Do not tell me that in this vast catacomb of knowledge there is nothing to aid my quest." He turned back to face the professor.

"You are yet to tell me your thoughts on the last book I gave you, Gaige," Lumire said, clearly trying to direct the topic to safer ground. "You are lucky to have the opportunity to read such a book. Three centuries ago almost every copy was burned, along with the author. The lord regent himself gave that book to the university."

"Professor, I have no interest in reading the philosophical musings of some ancient Brynthian, Arthur Weaver. You know the direction my interest lies."

"Now it is you who sound foolish, Gaige. You are hardly more than twenty years and you believe you know everything. Three centuries ago is not ancient. It is but a blink in the cosmic cycle of time. And the man's name was *Darcy* Weaver, not Arthur." Again Lumire shook his head. Gaige tried to speak, but the professor raised his hand. "Enough, Gaige. That will be enough.

"Let me tell you from all my years of experience and of teaching," Lumire continued, "a curse is a curse and cannot be lifted or altered. When one is taken by the plight of ghoulism, they are dead. Lycanthropy... they are dead. Vampirism... dead. Think of your history lessons. Think of Brynth and the Rata Plaga. For certain these plights of sorcery have no cure. Once changed, there is no return." Lumire scowled. "There is no bringing such a soul back. Such curses are final. That is scientific fact, and I must say your aggressive interest in the matter frightens me."

"I did not expect you to react like this," Gaige said as he limped away from the table into the vast, silent brilliance of the library. No one was there to see them, but he was glad the mask concealed his tears all the same.

He had always hated his birth parents' conservative idealism, and now he realized that the father he had chosen, the mentor he had trusted, was just the same. He bought all that the fearmonger sold and he cowered from the devil's domain —and in doing so, bowed down to its dark majesty.

Gaige had never felt so alone. Not even when the parents he had loved, though he hated their ideas, had succumbed to sickness within days of each other. Gaige and his crippled limb had survived, and buried deep in his box of regrets was the fact that he had never told them he loved them, he had only shown them his disdain.

His disappointment in Lumire changed nothing. He would still follow the path he chose, with no support; with the odds against him he would enter the beyond. He would unlock all the secrets he wanted to know. That was his purpose, the one he chose for himself. But his determination did not lessen the pain of his altered perception of his longtime mentor.

When he reached the doors, he looked above them at the tall painting of the lord regent. The frame was old and heavy, the gold marked with the green patina of age. The lord regent stood, long black hair sweeping his shoulders, dark eyes directed such that Gaige felt they were looking straight at him. The fire in those eyes looked like it could set the whole world ablaze. He wore a fine red coat with black epaulets and a glossy black trim on the high collar. Black threads wove an intricate design across the chest and down the abdomen, wolves on one side, ravens on the other, fur and feathers designed to give the impression of licking flames. At the bottom of the canvas were written the words "Insight be my Sword."

As Gaige pushed open the doors, his crippled left leg

ached more than usual, and with every step it screamed all the more. He passed by dark, empty lecture halls. The dim, lonely atmosphere almost swallowed him up.

The clicking of his cane on the marble echoed through the vast space like the ticking of a distant clock.

INTERLUDE

∼

This may be the most potent version of the oil I have developed thus far. Fredrick, the subject, has put on one stone of pure muscle in the past two weeks alone. His speed has increased; his endurance verges on remarkable, even for a mule of his fine breeding. His capacity of burden has increased by one hundred and twenty-five percent, and although I would not write it in a medical journal, just as personal note, I daresay I've noticed an increase in Fredrick's confidence.

I will be administering the oil to myself through intra-muscular injection twice every ten-day cycle, at one-eighth of Fredrick's dose.

Day 10: It is taking effect already. I decided to use a high-loading dose, and as a result I walked for the first time in my adult life about my apartments and down to the fountain in the center square without the use of my cane. But now, as I write this journal, I feel a sensation in my heart, not pain but more a weight on each beat.

INTERLUDE

Day 45: The dose is stable now. My body has increased its muscle tissue, including those muscles of my crippled leg. The sensation of a weight on my heart has not returned.

Day 70: Today I was capable—without the use of any other stimulants such as sanguinum—of running, even if at a slow pace, thrice round the entirety of the Fountain District. I do admit to some small embarrassment as city folk glowered at me distastefully as I passed, as if running and smiling were both crimes. Perhaps next time I will do the same but with my mask on and scalpels in my hands.

Day 322: Today that sensation of a small weight tugging down on my heart returned. This time it was accompanied by pain, treacherous pain.

~Gaige's Journal

CHAPTER TWO

THE DOCTOR

*L*umire was long dead now. He died before Gaige had the chance to prove him wrong, before he could say, "I did it. I brought them back. Ghoulism is not death. Lycanthropy is not death. Even to be cursed as Rata Plaga is not death, and death is not the only remedy." That was not all that Gaige wished he could have told the old professor, a man who for a decade had been his only friend, even after that night in the library.

Real death took Lumire, not a curse, not ghoulism, not Lycanthropy, just a deep black cancer in the gut. In his last weeks he even turned to witchcraft for help. It hadn't worked.

Gaige sometimes thought of that night at the university. He brought to mind who he had been at that stage long past, that passionate young man, dead and buried under hard gravel in the cemetery of his mind, the tombstone hard to see, so thick were the fogs of time.

Two decades will bog a man down.

The wheels of the old but sturdy cart, its wood etched with the nicks and carvings of adventure, squeaked over the wet cobbles of Villemisère. A long puddle ran like a river down the side of the road. The sewers must have clogged again. The water was putrid in smell and bilious in color. Gaige stared over the side of the cart; his reflection stared back at him. The lamp that dangled in the front of the cart illuminated Gaige's reflection and his long, wet red hair that fell wildly from the back of his doctor's mask like the feathers of a crimson bird. The back of the mask was not closed, but for a leather strap and a clasp that kept it fastened.

He looked away from the puddle and back ahead into the fog. His business was in the lower city, south, away from the Castle Misère and the university, away from his small apartments in the Fountain District, where he could cherish his loneliness with a hot cup of tea, a hot pipe, and a good book.

It had been raining an hour before, but it had stopped now and only a murkiness remained, hovering silently through the empty marketplace. The lanterns in the streets mingled with the fog, and together they cast glowing and mischievous forms upon the streets, while shadows danced on the walls of unlit houses. They were looming houses, tall, with thin, corridor-like apartments, and each one had a pointed roof and an ugly chimney that coughed up black smog. The roofs were like the silhouette of the jagged teeth of a lower jaw.

"Turn right," Gaige said to Randal, his driver, and they headed west down Krewl Street. The cool moisture worked its way under his coat and into the legs of his trousers, its chill biting at his aching, crippled leg. The leg was stronger than it had been; his chemistry experiments had seen to that. What had been tormented flesh and bone had developed muscle—an impressive amount of it—but the joints and bone beneath the alchemically attained muscle still ached horribly.

They passed the Chapel of His Burning Light, where a

blue-clad seeker holding a lantern talked idly with a priest in black robes as they walked down the front steps. And at the sight of the two men, the pain in Gaige's leg seemed to rage a bit more.

"Doctor!" called the seeker, his accent from Brynth, not Fracia. The priest nodded his head down a few degrees as well. Doctors and priests hardly got along, and Gaige even less so than most, especially after his work began curing the cursed. No exorcism necessary; just spilt blood and a formidable amount of alchemical concoctions. There was not much that couldn't be solved with science. Neither the priests nor the seekers liked that very much.

Gaige nodded back at them. He was scowling beneath his mask.

"Hold, hold if you would," called the seeker from the steps.

"Keep going," Gaige said to Randal.

"I don't think I should," Randal whispered as he pulled on the reins and slowed the cart. The seeker was taking his time coming down the steps.

"Why do I pay you, Randal?" Gaige asked as he grabbed the back of Randal's neck with a viselike grip and pulled him close. "Eh, Randal? I should just drive my own donkey cart from now on."

"I just think it is better not to be confrontational, is all," Randal said, putting his hands up in a demonstration of apology.

"Exactly. So you should have kept going. He is on foot."

"And we are in a *donkey* cart."

"May we have a word, doctor?" came the voice of the seeker from Gaige's right.

Gaige let go of the back of Randal's neck.

"About what?" Gaige said, turning around. Their jobs in some ways were similar; they both stood against the evils that all too often spawned from the dark things that only magic was responsible for. The difference between Gaige and the seeker was that Gaige fought the evils of magic by saving lives, curing curses, acquiring information on his patients through tracking, planning, reading, and talking as much as he could with those who could provide him with any insight into the cases on which he worked. Being saved, being cured, it always came at a price of blood and pain, but *life* was always the goal, and science always the means.

The seekers, on the other hand... they acquired information through torture; they cured curses with decapitations; they fought magic by kicking down doors of country girls' homes and burning them for witchcraft. They chased down pagan families in the woodlands with dogs and muskets, shooting some and leaving them to rot where they fell, and taking the rest to hang them from the city walls so that everyone could see Brynth was here, Brynth and God, the one true God, the Luminescent.

The choice was given to those of Fracia, to those who lived in Villemisère, just as many nations had been offered the choice before: kneel to the Luminescent, kneel to his vessel, his Imperial Majesty of Brynth, or hang from the gallows.

Since the coming of the lord regent, the seekers had not plied their vile deeds in Villemisère, but the lord regent did not govern all of Fracia or Brynth. Though he did not tolerate such deeds here, they happened elsewhere, and he could not change the deeds of the past.

"I would like to check that all your papers are in order, your documents concerning the substances you have with you for your practice," said the seeker.

"I only have one." Gaige peered out through his bird mask and locked on the glowing blue orbs in the seeker's square skull.

"One what?" the seeker asked, meeting his gaze.

"One paper," Gaige said, and took no action.

"For everything that you have with you?" The seeker almost looked pleased, certain that he had Gaige in some sort of trouble. "Well, I'd like to see that special paper." He smirked. "But doctor, you seem to have a good deal of... trinkets, and vials and whatnot back there. And, I must say, I have never seen such a mule. He is more muscular than any horse."

"Yes, Fredrick is quite the specimen. He is of royal stock all the way from Kallibar," Gaige lied.

The seeker moved closer to the chemically enhanced mule.

Then, feeling like pushing the man a bit further, because in the end, the seeker was still just a man, Gaige asked, "What do you care about my mule, anyway? You think he is a carrier or something? You think he has some sort of illegal, magical entity? Are you going to burn my mule on a pyre? Your kind is known for your fires."

"Hmm, I never knew the royalty of Kallibar was known for their fine mules," the seeker said. "And you know, doctor, your contemporaries, others who wear the mask... they don't have the cleanest hands, either. What was it they did in 1512 in Azria? They quarantined a whole village, then they cleansed it with fire." The seeker's eyes narrowed and his smile finally faded. "Your papers, doctor."

Gaige reached into the inside of his coat. The seeker struggled to appear relaxed, but he put a hand to the single-shot pistol on his belt. Gaige pulled out a small envelope and from within he removed a folded note. It was a writ of passage to move freely through Villemisère, whether on call or not. And it had the stamp of the lord regent.

"I only have one," he said again as he handed the seeker the letter.

The blue-hatted man opened it and his eyes went wide as he realized his mistake.

"My most sincere apologies, doctor, I had no idea—"

"Now you do," Gaige said as he snapped the note back and quickly folded it back up and into the envelope with dexterous fingers. Then he turned to Randal. "Please, Randal, do continue. We have time constraints."

Randal looked apologetically at the seeker, because Randal was a sap, and then he cracked the reins.

Gaige thought of the task ahead. He opened his coat and looked inside, though he knew everything was there—he had checked twice since they set out—but still it was calming to confirm yet again that he was prepared. Four glass syringes fortified with iron cages, and an iron pump; they were holstered in leather bands stitched to the inside of the coat. Two shots of sanguinum and two shots of adrenallys. The sanguinum was an intra-muscular shot that Gaige would inject into his thigh just before he got to work. The adrenallys was not for him, but for the patient. It would be needed to get her heart pumping after the surgery was complete.

They passed a crooked sign of rotting wood, the edges jagged and broken, the word "graveyard" carved in the center. The wheels creaked as they rolled down the wet cobbles of Villemisère, toward the bridge and the slums.

The slums were divided into two parts. There was low town, or, as the inhabitants called it, the Wastes, for the city's filth was brought there, both of the inanimate and the animate kind. The lepers, and the dung carts, the homeless vagrants and the corpses of all manner of dead things. The human bodies got taken past the Wastes and up past Enfer's Hill, where they would be brought past the graves to the feeding piles. These were mounds—sometimes hills—of human corpses, stocked with all of the city's fresh bodies to keep the cursed creatures, the spawns of sorcery, fed and away from the healthy. Only the wealthy were afforded the final luxury of a deep burial in a cast iron casket.

There were not always enough fresh corpses, not enough disease and murder at times to keep the monsters fed. When this was the case, certain individuals made a profit in the meat trade. Because when the beasts came wandering from the fringes, when they were chased by fire and sword, by gun and pitchfork out and away from the villages, they wandered to the city where people forgot the meaning of co-operation, and the sacred animal was the vulture.

The bridge was stone, covered in moss and fungi, vines reaching over the sides and dangling into the mucky green river that ran below. The excrement from the sewer drains in the slums all poured into that river. It was a short bridge, but the fog of that night was so dense Gaige could hardly see the other side.

"Proceed slowly, Randal," said Gaige, and Randal called, "Whoa, there," to the donkey, and the mutated mule slowed with a snort.

With every rotation of the wheels, the smell became fouler. It was the stench of shit and rot, the reek of death and the mingling of blood both fresh and crusted old. So powerful was the reek that one wretched smell became indecipherable from the next, and they merged together to create a pain in the sinuses that was the stink of hopelessness. Gaige was familiar with that stink. Day by day his tolerance of it slinked toward indifference. He had seen too much, suffered too much, and taken far too much to be quavered by a reek, even if it were the very aroma of hell.

When they reached the other side, Gaige looked over his shoulder and searched the tendrils of mist. Years of experience had taught him that in this place, both friend and foe kept watch before revealing their presence.

"Stop," he said to Randal.

Randal did, and took hold of the loaded musket that sat between the two of them. He stood in the cart and shouldered the gun. Gaige stepped down. He pulled his three-shot pistol from his hip and scanned his surroundings... Footsteps from the alley just ahead, no torch, just darkness. Gaige raised his pistol, waiting for whatever was to emerge.

INTERLUDE

∼

Dear Doctor De'Broullaird,

Your work is known to me. It has been for some time. I have a task that needs doing, a sensitive task, sure to only be carried out with the use of violence and at great risk to you, doctor. With great risk, as you've known since youth, I'm sure, comes great reward.

I ask you two things.

Firstly, should you accept my offer—I have no doubt you will— then take this writ of passage, marked by my very seal. It will allow you to move freely through the city, past curfews.

Second, meet with my agent, Briggs, at the Strangled Sturgeon. I daresay you know the one, dear doctor. Two nights from now, when sun goes down until it rises, he will wait there. I do assure you, you've been waiting for this opportunity your whole life. The chance to see beyond, to know the perfect pairing of science and that which only great mages dream, is the bait I dangle.

~ The Lord Regent of Villemisère

INTERLUDE

CHAPTER THREE

AMPUTATION

"Doctor, is that you?" came the sound of a familiar voice.

"It is I, Butcher. It is I." Gaige lowered his pistol. Randal sighed in relief and set down the musket.

"I was about to come looking for you with some of the lads. Devil's luck running into you like this. What brings you to my cesspool?" Butcher asked from the shadows.

"What always brings me to your cesspool, Butcher. I am on a job right now for the lord regent himself, and you would have had no need to come looking for me, for I was coming to you."

"You don't say? The lord regent sent you? Well, I suppose even the lord regent and his blue boys don't want to come trekking through these parts. Doubt they'd get a warm reception. Will you be needing anything from my stock?"

"I will be," said Gaige. "Come into the light where I can greet a friend."

From the shadows stepped forth a thing that had once been a man, and before that a boy. Butcher was six and a half feet tall, pale as the fog that levitated around his mutant muscled form. His veins bulged beneath his scarred skin, and his face was a thing of nightmares. His nose, his ears, his lips, and the skin of his face had been flayed off him as a boy. He'd survived. The result was the visage of death, a living skull.

It was Gaige who had saved him. Since then, they had been… friends.

"Why were you going to come looking for me?" Gaige asked.

"For a favor." Butcher smiled. He somehow had each and every one of his teeth, and they were straight and white. Animal white.

"I can grant a favor, so long as you leave me a few hours to spare before sunrise," said Gaige, returning the smile.

"Oh, you'll have plenty of time, doctor. It's just a small thing." Butcher's voice was strange; he hissed many of his words, for it was hard forming them without lips. "Follow me then, if you will," Butcher said as he turned and walked back into the shadow and the fog engulfing the alley from whence he had just come. As he always did when Butcher needed a favor, Gaige followed. Because do a favor for Butcher and he would always give you one back.

It was a scratching of each other's backs sort of deal. Gaige looked after Butcher and his gang, and for this Butcher and his gang watched Gaige's back whenever he came down to the slums, the times when his work brought him there, and that was often enough.

Gaige and Butcher walked. Gaige used his cane and was glad for a bit of a stretch after sitting on the cart for so long. Randal remained in his seat and followed the two of them, the cart just barely fitting the alley. They talked little the whole way; none of the three men cared much for chitchat. They passed droves of lepers, bowls for spare coin in front of them in a place where no coin could be spared. Gangs of ratty children ran around, grunting at each other like animals. Gaige saw a boy no older than ten run by, like the devil himself was pursuing him, a bloody knife in his hand. There was nothing unsettling about this, not in this place. The presence of a corrupt church made it worse, not better. Those who had coin to donate into the holy chalice once a week were the only ones who received the Luminescent's blessings, and, of course, the notice of his earthly disciples.

They passed vagabonds who intoxicated themselves by huffing fumes of foul things until they were just like the ghouls that were a constant looming threat—purposeless, defeated, ravenous. It was often hard to tell the difference in these parts between dead, living, and cursed.

"Welcome, as always," said Butcher when they arrived at his gang's hideaway. The Manor of Grime, they called it. Sometime ago, before the Wastes expanded to swallow chunks of the city and beyond, it had been a manor house to a lord. And now it was home to the Grimers. It was a tall house, with only two floors but ceilings of impressive height, so that from the outside one would guess at perhaps four or even five stories. Its brick was dark brown, the color of mud, and vines and green moss crawled up the walls on either side of the massive front doors. Painted on them were white skulls ten feet high cascading green poison tears from their empty eye sockets.

Two tall, hooded men, broad-shouldered but sickly thin, guarded the door. Each had a musket strapped to his back, several pistols around the waist, and on the thighs and in their hands they held blunderbusses that at close range could turn a man into chunks of meat.

They stood at attention and saluted Butcher. "Good to see you, doctor," said the man on the left. Gaige nodded in return.

"Sal, she is in poor shape," said Butcher when they walked into the atrium of the dilapidated manor house, a perfect home for a gang that referred to themselves by that ugly moniker of the Grimers. The walls had been maroon, or burgundy, perhaps, when a lord owned the house. Now they were shit brown in parts, and in others the wall had stripped away and the moldy, dying structure of the house was visible, beams of wood covered in green and blue fungi.

Sal—Saline—was one of the prostitutes that generated a good bit of profit for the Grimers. She was a popular girl, perhaps fifteen, and looked like she was pushing forty. She had half her teeth, and half her face had been beaten so badly once that the nerves had died, and so she was permanently drooping.

"Sal is tough," said Gaige, because she was. Anyone who lived among the Grimers was tough, especially those of the fairer sex. Gaige was acutely aware of the pressing engagement he had this night, but as a doctor and healer, he could not turn his back on the girl. As they climbed the creaking stairs to the second floor, Grimers saluted Butcher and said their hellos to the doctor as they passed. Gaige was always sure to say hello back. These were the type of men who when they showed you respect, you gave it back. Unless you enjoyed the prospect of having your eyes gouged out while another man twisted a knife in your liver. Besides, Gaige did respect them. They lived a hard life.

"I don't know this time." Butcher shook his head. "She was bit last night and the bloody infection has spread fast."

Gaige's attention sharpened. "Bit? By?"

"A customer. Some fuck from the Skulkers nipped her in the thigh." Butcher grimaced as he mentioned the name of the Skulkers, another gang that operated in the Wastes. They lived in the sewers, wore cloaks made of rat fur and masks of the rodents' skin. For the past year the Grimers and the Skulkers had held a fragile alliance, but that was liable to change at the slightest tilt of the knife. Or teeth.

They reached the room where Saline was being tended to, and the smell of rot increased just outside the door. Rotting, dying flesh; it was a hot smell, an evil smell.

"Randal?" Gaige asked, turning to his assistant, who had crept along behind them.

"I think I will remain outside, maybe downstairs at the bar, or a bit of dice," said Randal as he turned away from the room, his nose plugged with his fingers.

"Fuck off, then, Randal. I do hate when you linger," Gaige said, unsurprised by the young man's response. Randal nodded and was gone.

Gaige opened the door and stepped forth. The scent attacked him, but he did not waver. He had seen this a thousand times in the field. The failed war of independence fifteen years earlier had resulted in a rise of infected, rotting limbs. Gaige had honed his skills while the orchestra of agony had played around him. Two minutes for an arm. Three for a leg. And each time he got faster, and colder.

Saline was lying in a bed, the white cotton sheets befouled. Two Grimers were present, tending to the girl, both of whom were female, but as burly and hardened as any man. Saline was shaking violently beneath the sheets, and every step Gaige took, he pressed into that odor most sinister.

He pulled away the sheet. It stuck when it got past her waist, and he had to give it a bit of a tug to reveal the ailment.

Nothing too major. He opened the iron beak of his doctor's mask and reached into his coat pocket, removing a small vial. Within were the ground petals of moon's widow. Gaige opened the vial and sprinkled the petals onto Saline's open mouth to help dull her senses, then dropped a pinch more into the beak of his mask to help mask the smell.

Almost immediately the herbs took effect. Saline's thrashing and moaning decreased. She was naked, sweating profusely and suffering from racking shakes. Her entire thigh was rotting. The point of origin—where she was bitten—had spread and had now eaten through right to the bone. The flesh was black and maggots tunneled in and out of the wound, taking their fill.

Gaige looked at the older of the two women. "You applied the maggots?"

"I did," she said. "Fat lot of help it was."

"They slowed the infection. They're probably the reason she's still alive."

He continued his examination. Outside of that blackened region, the skin was fighting a losing fight and was burning a deep red, with blackened veins beneath. Through his gloved hand Gaige could feel the burning heat. He would have to amputate, and he would have to do so from the hip. Most other doctors would have decided it was a hopeless effort, and especially in these conditions. They would have turned to Butcher and explained that saving this girl was impossible. Well, saving her *was* impossible in the sense that Gaige was no savior, that if she lived it was to a life likely worse than death. *Maybe I should just kill her, give her too much of something. There is no coming back from this.*

"I don't know, Butcher," said Gaige.

"What don't you know?"

"If there is a point in this. I mean, what life will she have? She is a child, a prostitute, and now she will be legless."

"Save her. Let her choose. Like you did for me. Not everyone is as smart as you, doctor. Not everyone understands the blanket of suicide as you do."

Let her choose. That is fair, or as fair as it can be. "I will need my tools." He kept a set here, for he was here often enough. "I will need fire. I will need boiled water."

"You heard him," said Butcher, and the two women left the room to get Gaige his things.

Butcher nodded to Gaige when it was just them and the incoherent Saline in the room. "If she lives, do you think she will ever be able to work again?"

"You are a wicked man, Butcher. Repulsive, in body and mind."

The brute shrugged. "I didn't earn my name from being kind. She chose here, instead of out there."

"A lot of good that did her… To answer your question, let her choose." Gaige shrugged. "We both know you won't throw her out either way."

"How would I explain that to you if I did?"

Gaige turned back to his patient, and he thought of how Butcher had wandered through the Wastes looking for him, to help her.

Butcher and the two Grimers held the girl down and they gave her a thick rope to bite on. Gaige acted quickly. He boiled some of the moon's widow and forced Saline to drink. It was not enough to knock her out, but it took the edge off the bone saw's teeth as the instrument bit into her upper thigh and rocked back and forth. Saline bit the rope and frothed like a wild horse the whole time, and only when the leg was off, black, ruined blood oozing and spurting all the way through, did she finally pass out.

Ninety seconds, cut and sealed. That was all it took.

It was done.

Gaige applied mold to fight infection and bandages to stem the bleeding. The smell of the mold mingled with the infected limb, and the general wretchedness of the Wastes was so formidable that it fought its way into Gaige's beak and past the gentle-smelling ground petals of moon's widow.

One of the women brought him a bowl and soap and a relatively clean towel. She squeezed Gaige's arm in thanks.

He gave the Grimers a vial of a strong poultice that he had concocted himself; he only had one vial, for the ingredients were rare, but if anything could save Saline from another infection, it was that.

The chattering of Saline's teeth ticked off the seconds.

"I have a pressing matter, Butcher," Gaige said. Butcher handed him his cane, and motioned for him to follow. They left Saline's room, her delirious noises providing the ambiance of their exit.

Left through the atrium, right toward the east wing, another left, and through the library where the ceiling had a drip, an endless drip even on the rare days when not a single cloud hung in the sky above that melancholy city. Most of the books were damp and ruined, but sometimes when Gaige browsed a section of that vast chamber of now decaying knowledge, he found a book that had somehow endured against the pestilence that bayed so close by. There was no time to look for survivors on that day, so they went on through the high-ceilinged room, into the smoking lounge, the place most densely populated with Grimers puffing away on opium and injecting ground moon's widow. In the corner, a wild-eyed man in a shabby green military coat with long dreadlocked hair and a beard strewn with dirt shredded away on a violin, his harmony equal parts manic rage and collapsing depression.

Two doors led out to a small balcony that looked over the grimy river that cut Villemisère in two. On one side, their side, was the manor house and others like it all the way up until the bridge. Facing them across the river was a wall, wooden, but very thick. Not that it mattered. It was not built for defense, but just so the citizens of the suburbs and upper city, in the castle and university districts, need not look at the obscenity of the slums.

Beyond the wall, Gaige could see the tower of the university, and he thought of Professor Lumire. He thought of the riots, the student protests. This made him feel hollow, and he tried to push the ghosts away as he followed Butcher down the stairs from the balcony that led to the cellar. Because before the doctor could finish the night's business, he would need bait, and Butcher always had stock.

"Down we go," Butcher said, in fine good humor. He held a weak oil lamp in his hand as they descended. Gaige had been there many times before, but it never got any easier walking down those stone steps, the edges blackened, the centers worn from thousands upon thousand of footfalls, into the damp abyss below Butcher's fortress deep in the heart of the Wastes where the devil dared not go.

The tap of Gaige's cane echoed down the narrow, high-ceilinged hall at the bottom of the steps. When they finally reached the end, the air was thicker and fouler than it was above, and Gaige's leg screamed in demonic agony from all the steps.

"We have him," Butcher said, as they walked, a cruel smile on his leathery, skeletal face. His white teeth showed bright in the poor light of the lantern.

"You have who?" asked Gaige, his voice jittering from his lack of breath in the thick air, and fatigue from keeping up with Butcher's long strides.

"The mutt that bit Saline."

"Ah," said Gaige, and a shiver of sympathy crawled through him. There was no denying that the criminal was certainly a most lowly form of bastard. But what Saline had just suffered, Gaige was sure that Butcher would make this man suffer tenfold.

They reached the end of the hall and a rusted iron door barred their way. Gaige's and Butcher's breathing were the only sounds to be heard. The smell of copper, tangy and sharp, hung in the air. The meat room, Butcher called it. It was here that he brought stolen cadavers from the corpse wagon. It was here that he operated his "feed" business from, for when the free supply of bodies dwindled, the ghouls got hungry, the rats got hungry, the hounds, the Lycans—they all got hungry. Hungry ghouls made their way from the graves into the Wastes, and if they were hungry enough they went for the living.

Butcher prevented that from happening by taking the protection money of the citizenship and supplying food for the ghouls both from his own personal stock of fresh meat and by simply returning the pilfered corpses to the mounds he stole them from in the first place.

Butcher dug in a pocket for his key. He placed it in the iron door and gave it a turn. The heavy click of the lock echoed down the corridor.

Torches and lanterns on every wall painted the stone surfaces orange, and the shallow puddle of blood that covered the floor gleamed under the firelight. Stacked in the corners were hundreds of limbs, heads, and torsos. Gaige thought of the many times when he was a student that he had used Butcher's facility for his own medical research. It was for a greater good, he always told himself, and not some sort of sick curiosity.

He cared for the sick, the sick from the Wastes. He perpetuated this world by keeping its inhabitants alive.

Every time he returned to this place, though, it was harder and harder to convince himself that there was any good in his soul, that there was any good in the whole world. So he told himself nothing.

"Look at the pile, Gaige. He is still alive, the bastard," Butcher said, followed by a sound that was not laughter, just a terrible noise made in its place.

Gaige squinted, and then he saw the horror. In the mountain of mutilated flesh, there was a torso that still had a head, no limbs. Instead there were iron stumps, burned onto the severed stumps.

"The lads and I have been taking notes when we watch you perform, doctor. It is a marvel, what a man can take before he dies."

Gaige saved people. Butcher murdered them. But to a man like Butcher, perhaps they were one and the same.

He walked toward the wriggling thing. The eyes were burned out and the mouth was sewn shut. A faint moaning came from the wretch, and at the sound Gaige hated Butcher, he hated that damned city, and he hated himself for the job he still had to do in those dark hours of the morning before the sun rose.

He twisted the handle of his cane, from it drew his sword, and in a surgically accurate and swift motion he slit the mutilated man's throat. Blood shot from the wound more fiercely than it should have, and Gaige knew Butcher's men had fed their toy powerful elixirs to keep his heart beating as they chopped him up.

"A bit too far, Butcher, a bit too far," Gaige said, his voice hollow and without any real reproach.

Butcher stepped beside him. "Nothing is too far in this place, no fate too cruel. One day I will pay for all that I have done"—he gestured at the limbless torso—"just as this shit pile did, and I am ready for that price. I am ready for anything, because in truth, I have come to believe that this is all just some horrid dream, a horrid dream without limits to its depravity." Butcher indicated the heaps of death around him. "How can this be real? How can any of this be real, doctor?"

Gaige did not answer; he turned away from the corpse with the iron stubs to look at Butcher, who was staring into a torch on the wall. Gaige could see into his eyes and he saw a great fear in them, a great and endless fear.

"I am going to need something fresh if you have

anything," Gaige said, trying to move things along. The urgency of his mission weighed on him now.

Butcher turned from the fire on the wall and looked at Gaige. He made that noise again, the one that replaced laughter. The fear was still in his eyes.

"You can take him." Butcher pointed to the iron-stumped horror as his feral white smile grew. "For you are the one who just slaughtered him fresh."

INTERLUDE

∼

Note to self: Never again, not ever under any circumstance administer two doses of sanguinum, or mix sanguinum with any other alchemical substance of equivalent, or antagonizing value.

Symptoms: vomiting, haemolacria... my heart is going to burst.

—*a note scrawled into Gaige's journal by a shaking hand*

∼

CHAPTER FOUR

THE CONTRACT

The wind howled.

"Easy there, Fredrick, easy there," said Randal in a soothing tone to the mule to keep him from getting spooked.

Fredrick had never gotten spooked before, because Fredrick was chemically altered to be fearless. Randal was not. And so Gaige believed that Randal said this as a way of calming himself before the violence began. It never worked.

The wind howled again, and the things that lived among the shallow graves and sunken tombs howled back.

Randal gave Gaige a weak look, as if asking without words if they could please just stop. Gaige knew better than to allow this, because whenever Randal was given a moment, he started developing severe cases of second thoughts. Though Randal was next to useless, he was better than no second gun at all.

"I gotta fuckin' piss," said Randal. "I gotta fuckin' piss bad."

"Give me the reins. Piss over the side," Gaige said.

"The wind. I'll piss on myself." Randal shot him a glance. "I don't want to interfere with the ritual."

"Don't call it that." Gaige growled as he cuffed Randal on the side of the head. "What have I told you about calling it that?" He paused, tamping down his fury. "It is a surgery, a medical procedure, not a ritual of sorcery. Now piss off the side, or piss in your pants, or wait until we get to the location we seek."

"Which is where, exactly?" Randal asked, despite Gaige's tone.

"We will mark the bait and put it on the tree that the client specified," Gaige said, more to himself now than to Randal.

"How did the client get all that stuff for the rit... I mean surgery, anyway? The scent of the man that broke off the engagement with the afflicted? How did he bottle the man's scent? That is what you told him to do, right? Get you a bottle of the man's scent?"

"Eavesdropping again, Randal?" Gaige asked without surprise. Randal possessed the stealth of a dawn rooster. "I didn't tell him to do anything. I told his man that it would be helpful if they could get me the scent of a man that has wronged the patient horribly, and it must be a man she shares a close history with. I did not actually hope that they would provide it, but in my long career I suppose that eventually, everything will happen. So for once, I will not need to track the patient down. The patient will come to us. How the client obtained for me fifteen vials of the man's blood, sweat, and tears is not our question to ask."

"Strange thing to say for a man hellbent on discovery, no?" Randal grumbled.

"Obvious question to ask for a man who is a curious idiot," said Gaige.

"How? How so? You are an asshole, you know that? It is

because you are a doctor, so I forgive you. But is curiosity not the foundation of discovery—"

Gaige put up his hand, silencing Randal's questions.

As if summoned, a low-branched willow manifested from the fog. On its dead arms clung an unkindness of ravens, all of them fine specimens of their species, wide, tall, and menacing. There was an uncanny intelligence in the way they observed, and an impossible union of movement, each head turning in unison, their eyes locked on him. Something nagged at the edges of his thoughts, like he had seen them before, on a tree like this, and it was burning, but the ravens were left unsinged.

He blinked and the thought drifted away.

Gaige pointed Randal toward the tree, off the path, past forty or so sporadically placed tombstones and up a small hill.

"How can you be sure?" asked Randal, unease in his voice, then he dropped his tone to a whisper. "They're ominous birds, silently perched, as if they're the audience waiting for a coming show."

"I am sure because we were told to find a tree and there is no other tree. Stop the cart," Gaige said. Randal did, and they stepped down onto the narrow dirt road that ran through the graves. Gaige limped to the back of the cart, which held the bait and the iron casket that Gaige used to transport the patients after their surgeries. Dead or alive.

His leg was aching, screaming at him, and he was glad it was time, for the injection would ease his pain. He opened his coat and took out a syringe filled with the amber fluid that was sanguinum.

"Why don't you ever let me try any of that fighting juice?" asked Randal as he began loading the five muskets in the back of the cart.

"I thought you had to piss," Gaige said, postponing the

shot. He never took a dose in Randal's immediate vicinity, for he feared he might lash out at him before he got the effects of the sanguinum under control.

"I do. But I'm curious. I just wanted to see you take it."

"Do you know what happened to the last man who had your job, Randal?" Gaige asked, as he glowered at his driver. "I'll tell you. He had a similar curiosity about the sanguinum. He had it for the adrenallys and the moon's widow, and the Liquanum and the Heccatille, and all my other secrets, Randal." He paused. "Go piss."

Randal looked at Gaige, his expression both interested and wary. "What happened to him?"

"He's dead, Randal, and it was his own fault," Gaige said, not allowing even a drop of remorse to color his tone.

Randal waited, and when Gaige said nothing more, he finally turned away and hefted the limbless, iron-stumped bait, mumbling that he only got paid to be a driver.

"The vials," Gaige called after him.

Randal returned, set down the bait, retrieved the vials of scent, set them carefully in the pocket of his coat, and then hefted the bait once more.

"Have a care with the vials," Gaige said.

"I'm not a child or a fool," Randal said.

"Debatable on both counts."

Randal walked toward the tree with the ravens, muttering about bait and piss and doctors who had no respect.

When he was gone, Gaige looked again at the glorious amber liquid before he jammed the needle into his once ruined left leg. It was ruined still, but under the effects of the sanguinum, it was less ruined. He pressed down on the plunger and he thought he might be sick from the severity of the pain that oozed its way into him. It felt like a tide of poison blasted in all directions from the point of the injection.

Then the pain in his leg faded; his heart rate escalated. He began to sweat, bile burning the back of his throat until he fell to his knees and heaved and threw up.

At length he got to his feet, the movement explosive, bursting up like a great bird of prey. It was not merely that he moved as if his leg hadn't been crippled for the miserable, seeming eternity that was his life, but he had the mobility and capacity that would put to shame a trained sportsman. He could feel every volt of energy shooting through his tendons, and in his vision the world seemed to have been befallen by a redness, so that the gray fog was tinged with crimson, the grass that had been dark green was blackened, every blade of it rimmed in the finest line of red.

His sense of smell changed, not simply intensified but focused, homed in on blood. He could smell Randal's fear close by, and it was more significant than usual. He could smell the blood of the ravens on the willow. There was no fear in them.

Gaige picked up the hangman's rope from the back of the cart, approached quickly, his sword cane in his belt now, passing Randal and snatching up the bait as he did.

"Your poor pace is a worrisome blemish on your character, Randal," Gaige said in passing. Randal said nothing; he just maintained his pace, despite the relief of his burden.

Even when Gaige reached the foot of the tree and tossed the hefty slab of human meat hard upon the exposed roots of the willow, the ravens did not move. They did not caw. And the scent of their blood did not change.

The doctor was not an easy man to unnerve, for in his very particular line of work one must always remain stoic, indifferent to the terrors that reality has to offer. But those staring black-eyed avian watchers beneath the red-clouded sky perched on the dead willow painted the very image of dread; it was the promise of violence, and as Gaige looked at the birds he thought of the lord regent's man's words: *"She will come to a willow. It will be marked, this tree. Marked with ravens. She will come."*

"I'm coming up there," Gaige said to the birds as he tied one end of the hangman's rope around the bait's neck, and threw the other over the lowest tree branch. Still they did not move.

With the bait twisting in the wind, Gaige grabbed the lowest branch and swung up, then stilled, his gaze on the narrow road.

"What was that, doctor?" Randal asked from a few meters away.

"Hand me one of the vials of scent," Gaige demanded. "Careful now."

Randal was at the bottom of the hill and reached one of his hands into his deep coat pocket.

"Got one right here, if I can just…" Randal tried to do three things at once, searching for a thin glass vial in his deep, likely stuffed coat pocket, trying to walk up the hill to Gaige, and looking up at the ominous ravens perched on the willow instead of focusing on the low gravestone in front of him.

As a result he tripped on the gravestone, a stupid look on his face while he fell, his hand still in his pocket. He crashed hard into the ground. There was a hardly audible crack and Gaige winced as he heard it.

It was not a bone—it was the vial.

He could smell the blood that was supposed to be on the bait, the bait with the noose around its neck.

Randal pulled his hand from his pocket and stared at it.

"I've gone and cut myself. Bloody thing cracked and cut me." It was clear by the driver's tone that he at least somewhat understood the greater implications of what his lazy attention had just brought upon him.

"Oh, Randal, you have really fucked things now," Gaige said. *I can still fix this. He may not have to die.*

Gaige sniffed the air and caught it: the scent of infectious rage, his patient, the Lycanthrope.

The information given by the client's man was correct.

She was coming. She was close.

And Randal was still on the ground.

"Quickly, you damned fool. She is nearly upon us. Arm yourself." Gaige's words finally snapped Randal's focus away from the wound in his hand, his death mark, and sent the driver sprinting with all the effort his young legs could muster toward the muskets on the cart.

Gaige leapt from the tree, and although he felt no pain now, he knew he would pay for these acrobatics later. He drew his sword and his pistol, crouched low, and hid among the tombstones on the hill beneath the tree.

Randal got up onto the cart and shouldered one of his muskets.

Gaige sensed the Lycanthrope coming closer.

This was not supposed to happen like this, Randal, but that is on you.

The last driver had died with malice and treachery in his mind. Randal would die for idiocy. It did not sit well with Gaige.

"Doctor? Where are you? I don't want to be the fucking bait. That's what I am now, isn't it? That's what the broken vial made me?" Randal cried out as he quickly twisted side to side, looking into the fog for any sign of the doctor or the patient. He was alone with Frederick the fearless, the very mule of stoicism.

Gaige clenched his fists. Every bit of his humanity demanded that he go and save Randal. Every bit of his professionalism demanded that he stay put and see the job through. If luck was on his side, the end of this night would see him do both.

Luck was rarely on his side.

"Shut up. Get a hold of yourself. When she appears, make the first shot count. And don't fire early." Gaige scuttled low, head beneath the wooden crosses and slabs that served as headstones. He paused, taking cover behind one of the large, towering gravestones made of obsidian, monuments to the ones before, thousands of years before. "We must adjust now, because of your incompetence."

"It was an accident!" Randal protested.

"There are no accidents," Gaige responded, his every sense attuned to the sounds and smells and whispers of the night.

Enter the beast.

She came at the back of the cart from the fog at such a speed that the vapor shredded and rippled around her. She barreled on all muscle-heaped fours toward Randal, the subject of her fury, thanks to the scent now permeating him from the contents of the broken vial. Gaige had never seen such a Lycan, more a cross between a humanoid and a shaggy golden dog than a wolf.

With his dexterity enhanced, his hands flashed in a blur as he drew from his coat the second syringe of sanguinum and jammed it into his leg. He frothed from the mouth and bit down so hard his gums bled, but the odious effects he had experienced earlier never came with the second dose. The needle came out, the syringe was tossed, and he rose from the graves. With equal speed he charged to intersect his patient.

Randal fired, too early. The musket cracked and the shot was true. The patient's golden fur streaked red as the musket ball ripped through her shoulder and out the back. Yet she was not slowed.

Gaige moved faster.

Not fast enough.

She leapt for Randal, and with a strike of such speed it was nearly invisible she clawed him in the gut, blackened nails digging deep, and hurled him from the cart.

Gaige was steps behind her. He raised his three-shot pistol and fired all three rounds into the patient's back before she could rip the incapacitated Randal to shreds. This was enough of a threat to turn her around to face the doctor. He tossed the pistol down and slipped his right hand into the brass knuckles he wore on his belt. The Lycan lunged and slashed a claw. Gaige quick-stepped under the strike and landed a shallow slash on the patient's belly. She was bleeding profusely already from the four gunshots. He would have to act quickly if he was going to keep her alive.

In the background, he could hear Randal sobbing. He didn't let himself listen.

The patient's fury heightened once again, and this time *he* was her passion. She slashed out thrice. The third caught Gaige's arm, shredded his flesh, and spun him around. The next strike opened up his back and sent him sprawling to the ground, nearly splitting his head on a tombstone. He rolled away from a fatal downward strike. For less than a second he looked up into the red sky, and then she was on him, fetid breath blowing hot gusts in his face. He dropped his sword and grabbed the beast by the wrists before it could sink its claws into him.

Her snapping fangs came close. Gaige tilted his head back, then jerked his head forward and rammed the iron beak of his mask into the patient's throat. She gave a strangled howl. Gaige planted his feet against her solid abdominal wall, and with all his might he kicked her back, blood coughing up from her throat.

Surging to his feet, he began backing toward the cart, toward the still-loaded muskets that lay by the iron casket.

The Lycanthrope understood the threat. She charged. Gaige stepped right to avoid a left claw, but with imperceptible speed the patient twisted back around and razor claws gouged into his right thigh. The sanguinum was piping hot through his veins, and even as he saw the claws cut him he did not feel it. Not yet.

He pressed forward, and with his brass-knuckled fist he struck the golden-haired beast across the mouth. She was stunned, and could not rally to avoid the second blow, a swing with bad intention. The knuckles cracked hard against skull and the blow echoed. She evaded a third strike, stumbling back out of his reach.

Gaige could not feel the pain from his wounds; the sanguinum saw to that. But that claw had scored deep into his right leg, and between that fresh immobilizing wound and his crippled left leg, it was becoming increasingly difficult to stand, chemical enhancements or no.

"Just lie down. Quit," Gaige growled.

The Lycan's eyes were a gray blue, glinting with red in Gaige's vision. Her golden hair swayed in the wind. Gaige could smell her blood; he could smell her defeat. She growled back at the doctor and, close by, the until-then-silent ravens perched on the willow began to caw as if in approval.

She had lost a lot of blood, lost it fast, so her next strike was slow. Gaige was bleeding, but not as badly, and his double dose of sanguinum was reaching its peak.

He evaded a claw, a snap of the teeth, a claw, another, then a wild shoulder charge, the last mistake. Gaige pirouetted to the side then with his wobbling legs rooted as best they could, the doctor twisted through his core and hammered the Lycan in the ribs with a dropping blow.

She sprawled on the ground fighting for air. She half

snapped, half licked at the air, hoping that something in it would grant it the energy to fight on. Gaige could see in the defeated eyes of the cursed that nothing was to be found. Sorcery had lost, to a *mortal* man and his medicine, and his science.

Gaige let out a shrill caw, the sound of some terrible, predatory black bird, and grabbed hold of the mane of hair and began wrestling the patient to the cart. She was heavy, the ground was muddy, and their fight had made it more slippery still. Gaige fell and the Lycan took the opportunity to try and crawl away.

"Oh no you don't. This is for your own good," Gaige said through heavy breaths as he wearily pulled himself back to his feet using a gravestone for support. He stumbled back to the patient. She snapped at him when he reached out to again try and drag her to the surgery table. A final administration of brass fist served as the needed dose of anesthesia.

"Randal? Are you alive?"

A piteous moan was the only reply.

"Stay that way!" He couldn't go to him. Not yet. He had a patient to cure, a task to finish. He must see this to the end.

In the distance, the things of the graves were rising, roused by the bloodshed and the whimpers of a dying man grinding through the foggy sky along with the doctor's grunts of reckless effort and the snarling of the golden-haired Lycanthrope. They would be having a feeding frenzy if Gaige did not hurry.

Randal groaned. Somewhere beneath the raging blood that boiled from the sanguinum, somewhere in his mind, there was a young Gaige De'Brouillard. This younger, calm-blooded self wept for Randal, and he yelled at the current Gaige, *"Help him, you bastard!"*

Gaige reached down and grabbed the patient by her golden ankles above razor-clawed feet, and he dragged her the rest of the way to the cart. If he was fast enough he could still save both. He had to be fast enough. He focused his gaze, chin over his shoulder, on Fredrick the Fearless that stern mule, easily grazing there by the road amongst the torrent of violence that had just befallen the earth around him.

"Doctor!" Randal whimpered, the sound turning Gaige's heated blood to ice.

"Don't yell, Randal. Just shut up. Listen to the sounds of the night, the music of the graves." *Be silent. Be still. Sleep before the ghouls find you.*

Gaige tripped up his step, forcing him to look away from the donkey and back at the ground in front of him. Deep crimson streaks of blood were swathed across the dirt from where *their* struggle had ended, and it just became the *doctor's* struggle.

Gaige tossed the remaining four muskets off the back of the cart and, despite it costing him a good squirt of his own blood shooting out of that cruel leg wound, heaved the patient into the cart, then himself.

Don't let him die.

Gaige winced.

The patient has priority. Randal knew this.

Did he? Did he really?

Gaige opened the iron casket in the back of the cart, then stuffed the patient inside, quickly arranging her into anatomical position. She was losing body mass rapidly. She was dying, and so was the disease. Her hair-fur was shedding off the body. As her snout shrank away, her doglike teeth fell away too. He punched down hard on the lever at the base of the iron casket and it sprang up to the height of an operating table for the doctor when he got to his feet.

He opened his bag of tools and medicines that were already at the foot of the seven-foot casket.

The first thing he took note of was the single loaded

syringe of purple liquid that was moon's widow. There was only one left, because Gaige had been known to use them on the wrong occasions, creating hard choices for himself in situations much like the one he was in currently.

He decided, ultimately, that he needed it more. He couldn't save anyone if he bled out here on his feet. He ripped away the fabric of his already torn sleeve and tied it around his thigh to slow the bleeding—his veins were already bulging from the struggle and the sanguinum, so it was of little difficulty for him to find a vein.

The pump went down and the purple liquid oozed into him. The red mood that had been hanging over the world dissipated.

Indigo-blue and violet hues streamed through space. The doctor's hands became steady. Despite the sounds of the dreaded things lurking in the close beyond, his soul was at ease.

The patient was fading as quickly as the disease. Death would take them both free of discrimination. The doctor grabbed a vial—silver dust with Lupus-bane and human blood comingled inside—and then a long needle. Gaige opened the vial and pulled the iron plunger of the syringe up. It filled, too slowly.

The patient writhed side to side in her death throes. She was human now, a blonde young woman, of prime athletic anatomy, an overdeveloped deltoid on the pulling arm suggesting… *the practice of a bow, perhaps? Masterful practice, by the looks.*

Who are you to the lord regent?

"This is going to hurt, then the beast will be gone for good," he said.

He pressed his left forearm across her chest, leaning his weight on her to still her struggles as best he could, and brought his hand down to stab the long needle into her heart. The Lycanthrope within screamed out one last time, the sound a devil makes as it gets sucked back into the fire. Beneath his black bird's mask, Gaige smiled at the sound. The smile faded as he heard a horrific sucking gurgle from behind, the sound of a throat being ripped open by a ghoul.

He thought of nothing but the patient before him. He reminded himself that the lord regent had ordered Briggs to stress a single thing.

"The patient must live," Briggs had said.

"Or no reward?" Gaige had asked, cynical.

"The patient must live, doctor," Briggs had said again, his glowing blue eyes peering from just below the brim of his hat. "The stakes are greater than you know. It is not your life, or hers, or mine, or even the lord regent's at risk. She *must* live."

The doctor worked alone, not letting himself think of Randal's loss, maintaining speed. Burning was faster than stitching, and so he set to that quickly, using his oil torch, an iron canister that pumped oil by the pressure applied via a trigger below the nozzle. The oil then sprayed a mist into a match lit before it. The result was a thin, powerful blast of flame. Gaige applied its heat to metal instruments and sealed up all the patient's leaks. Her mouth opened and every muscle in her neck tensed like it would rip, but she did not have the force to scream, so she did so silently.

When it was done, Gaige slammed shut the lid of the iron casket and stomped the pedal of the mechanism on the floor of the cart, and the casket dropped back down to foot level.

Gaige looked out into the graves and the blanket of mist. Not fifteen feet away, Randal lay dead, his guts out on display as he was consumed by the first of the ghouls. The doctor had not realized how close they had gotten. And all around he was beginning to see their silhouettes form in the fog.

It was too late to do anything now. It did not matter that

it hurt to see it; it did not matter that he wanted to run at the cursed beings and cut them with his cane. Because he could gut ten of them, he could be drenched in their blood, rancid, sick red droplets beading and falling off the tip of his beak, but the next ten would be there before the first ten lost their hearts or heads, and he would die. And so the patient would die locked in her iron casket.

So he stepped over from the back of the cart into the front and sat down, and he lifted and cracked Fredrick's reins.

"Come, Fredrick, before we are overwhelmed," Gaige said to the donkey, then cracked the reins again. The mutant steed's muscles burst into gear and they were off, as fast as Fredrick could go.

He thought only of the address now, the estate in the country—Coldcreek Manor—the place where he had been instructed to meet the lord regent, and to bring the patient for further care and recovery. He thought it funny, for as a young man, despite his parents' and doctors' warnings, he used to go for long country rides. The point he would always reach was Coldcreek Manor, and he would sit at the top of the hill and look down to the sheltered valley where the house stood, white brick catching the sun. It had looked like an architectural cross between a Brynthian fortress, with a solid central structure, and a Fracian villa, with sloped roofs that stretched out over the luxurious balconies with banisters of white stone. He had loved that house in the first half of his life. It had been a dream, a fantasy, a perfect jewel set among manicured lawns and bright flowers. A place that didn't belong in this dark world.

Years later he had heard the rumors that the house had been built over top of catacombs, vast underground burial chambers of an ancient race that had housed both the living and the dead beneath the earth.

Gaige had not gone for many years.

Hours and many miles had passed when for a moment he dozed off, the drugs wearing off and exhaustion taking hold. He jerked awake and thought Randal was beside him. He extended the reins for the young man to take.

But Randal was dead.

Guilt whipped at Gaige's soul. He opened a box where he stored all his regrets and shame, and he added this to the overflowing contents.

The outcome of this night was not the storybook ending he would never admit he had secretly hoped for. He hoped for it every time. But that was not something a man versed in reality said; not out loud, anyway. So he swallowed that taste of disappointment that he knew better than anything, and he reminded himself that while a young man had died a painful, but relatively quick death, a young woman was saved. So, in some sense a scale was balanced and all was fair, all was natural.

But the heaviness in his limbs, the numb tingling in his fingers, and the weight on his heart that threatened to crush it were not natural. They were all sequelae of the drugs, worse than he had ever experienced before. He wondered if he would survive them.

It was another hour before he reached the hill on the road that looking down on the valley at Coldcreek. It was as he remembered, bold and light in the dark green country and forest. A blue river ran just beyond, and Gaige was surprised that he only remembered the river again now. There was the sound of flapping wings, and ravens—ones of the same size as those on the tree in the graves—flew overhead, past him. They took their perch on Coldcreek's balcony, and they stared out at Gaige, up the hill.

A vise constricted around his heart. Pain lanced his left shoulder and arm.

He stared back at the birds, and they were the last things he recalled before the effects of his drugs finally wore off completely. Exhaustion set in to the fullest. His lids drifted shut. He jerked them open, and realized he was slumped over, his cheek against the wooden seat.

Again, his lids drifted down. Against his will they were closing. So close to his destination he could not fight off sleep. The pressure on his heart was unbearable, the pain radiating down his left arm and up his neck even worse.

He could feel each beat of his heart, his pulse stuttering.

And he knew fear that he would not live to see the beyond the lord regent had promised.

INTERLUDE

∽

Since the dawn of man there have been sorcerers and their beasts, in every corner of every cave, in the depths of the sea, waiting to rise one terrible night beneath the moon and walk upon solid earth. They dwelt in the forests, and the mountains, and for thousands of years they dominated us, brutalized and fed upon us. Man went below the surface, hid away, and strengthened himself so that one day he could return to the light on the surface. Return and unleash his vengeance on those dreadful things he had cowered from in terror for so long. It is up to us, as the men and women of today, to do what the old ones did, the ones who came out from the caverns and pushed the fiends aside to make way for the age of man. The greatest age.

-Dante Varron, the first seeker

∽

CHAPTER FIVE

DREAMS OF BEYOND

The doctor's eyes opened. A hard surface pressed against his back, or perhaps he pressed against the surface. A drowsy orange light stung his pupils. He blinked and blinked again. His mouth tasted like he'd licked a ghoul's foot.

Randal was dead.

The girl was alive.

At least, she had been last he looked.

The drowsy glow came from the chandelier above. He was sitting at the head of a long, empty dining table, upright, as if he had been in the middle of meal. Across the table at the opposite end sat a broad-shouldered man. His straight, dark hair was swept back from his forehead and fell to his shoulders. His fair skin was a contrast to his dark hair. He wore a red coat embroidered with the symbols of ravens on one half and wolves on the other.

"Lord regent," Gaige croaked.

"Ah, doctor, you're back." He was very still, his eyes dark and fathomless. "I guess it worked. At times I impress even myself." The lord regent smiled.

"I must have passed out," Gaige said. "You found her? She is stable?"

At this the lord regent began to laugh.

"You truly are impressive, doctor. Tell me, how do *you* feel?"

Gaige didn't trust the lord regent's good humor. He sincerely questioned why he had just awoken upright at an empty dining table. Gingerly, he shifted on the chair. He should have been feeling a hellish throb in his chest, another in his ruined leg, and a third in his injured good leg. The absence of agony was unsettling.

"What did you give me?" Gaige ran a hand over his left leg, and he extended it. No aches, just a loud creak, like an old door hinge.

"You died, doctor," said the lord regent, still smiling.

"I died?" Gaige's heart rate began to increase… Or at least it should have with his rising anger. But it didn't. Gaige put his hand to his chest.

He could feel nothing. Not just an absence of pain, but an absence of his pulse.

He put his hand to his neck, to the carotid pulse. *Nothing.*

"What's happening?" Gaige stood, and although there was no pain he did so slowly, with an immense stiffness, as if he had not risen for days.

"By the time I got to you, doctor, you had been dead already for nearly ten minutes. No alchemy for that, I'm afraid." The lord regent stood from his chair.

Gaige took a deep breath. It wasn't the first time vile dreams had haunted his rest after he self-administered the drugs.

"You aren't dreaming," the lord regent said as he crossed the vast dining room and exited through a doorway at the back. "Come along."

Curious, Gaige followed. He walked, stiff-limbed and creaking, feeling like a ghoul with his shuffling gait. After a few steps he began to gain some pace as the stiffness eased.

"If I was dead, how am I alive?" Gaige snarled at the red-coated man's back.

The lord regent turned around.

"I don't have time for the long version, so I'll give you the short one. You died. I did not expect you to die. Right outside the point of your quest's completion, no less. I was hoping you would return with her, you would stay here to recover from your wounds, and I would be able to explain what comes next. However, your addictions—"

"I suffer from illness. My line of work is physical—"

"I was not condemning you, doctor. But the fact remains that your addictions killed you, stopped your heart dead. Conveniently for you, and for my goals, I possess certain... abilities."

"Abilities?" Gaige asked, already suspecting the answer, one he was quite certain he would not like. Of course, dead was worse than displeased, so he made no complaint.

"Abilities of a magical nature. I've dabbled in necromancy. Not much, I do admit, and that is why we don't have much time."

Horror rained down on the doctor then. He was... the reanimated dead. Not a ghoul that might be cured from its cursed state. No, he was a transient ghost that would soon fade. When the spell wore off, he would return to a decomposing corpse.

"If you possess such power, why send me to that graveyard this night? Why not attend to the task yourself? And why make me this... this..."

"Walking corpse?"

Gaige glared at him.

The lord regent glanced back over his shoulder and laughed. "As I said, doctor, I only dabble in necromancy. You don't have long, not in this world. I made you this way because I need you still. You are of no use to me dead. As to your other questions, the answers will do you no good now."

Briefly did Gaige consider sitting back down, refusing to follow, refusing to play the lord regent's game. But he had no wish to be a dead man, or rather, a *more* dead man. And he had every wish to discover this beyond the lord regent had promised him as his prize.

He said so, and the lord regent replied, "Then by all means, follow me."

Follow Gaige did, and he noticed that for a dead man he was particularly spry.

They walked some distance until they reached a vast room, twice the size of the dining room, with a high-domed ceiling. The room was dominated by pillars of differing heights, and on each was displayed an artifact such as Gaige had never even imagined. So much knowledge, all in one place. Ancient stones and pieces of magnificent armor, and blades marked with symbols of some unknown time.

"From the catacombs beneath Coldcreek," the lord regent offered. "The catacombs of lost knowledge."

Gaige felt a stirring within himself, an uncontrollable urge to reach out and touch one. He spun a full circle, wanting to touch them all, each one giving off a unique sensation of temptation. And so he did: he touched the closest artifact, the hilt of a curved black sword crafted of a substance not unlike obsidian.

When his fingertips rested on the pommel, his vision blackened for an instant, and when it returned he was with the lord regent no longer.

In his hand was the obsidian sword, and he was standing in a stone hallway, statues of eyeless, naked swordsmen every twenty feet. Behind him stood men in black armor. To his right, men in black armor, and more to his left. A sound came from down the hall, a hall so deep that the end could not be seen. There was only blackness. From the blackness emerged silver-furred shapes, torches in clawed bestial hands, fangs and red eyes burning in the darkness.

The men behind Gaige roared cries of battle in an ancient tongue, and Gaige raised the black sword. In the same tongue as the warriors at his back, Gaige roared, "Slaughter the beasts."

With a cry, Gaige stumbled against the pillar and dropped the sword with a clatter. The stone hallway was gone. No silver-furred beasts charged. No warriors stood at his back.

"Careful, doctor," the lord regent warned. "That is not where I'm trying to send you."

Gaige stared incredulously at the lord regent, then back at the sword. This had to be a dream, all this. It all defied logic, defied reason. But what he had just seen had been real; he could still feel the heat, the fear, the fury of the men behind him. He could hear the sound of the beasts as they came forth.

"Explain. Explain everything. My one purpose is to gain knowledge. To understand. And right now, I understand nothing."

"Why must you understand?" the lord regent asked.

"My life. My suffering. Everyone's suffering," Gaige snarled. "I need answers to fix it. Don't you see? Our world, our broken world... I need the answers."

"Scientific answers."

"There are no other kind."

"And yet here you stand," the lord regent said. "A dead man walking. A dead man rapidly running out of time. So I ask, doctor, what will it be? Answers, or a quest undertaken on faith?"

Gaige stared at him, everything he believed, everything he knew screaming for answers. And yet… "The quest," he said.

The lord regent nodded. "Take off your mask," he said. "I *see* you, Gaige. You have no need to hide anymore."

Gaige stared at him through the eyeholes, as he had stared at the world from behind this wall for so many years now. And then he reached up and undid the clasp.

"Hello," said the lord regent with a smile. And then, "Stay close." For the rest of the way through the massive hall, Gaige kept his eyes focused on the lord regent's coat, forcing himself to ignore the siren's song of the artifacts.

They reached a bookshelf that was two stories high, and as long as a house. The lord regent removed a volume—*The Indisputable Science of Goodness* by Darcy Weaver—replaced it with another tome, and then took out three volumes to the right of Weaver's book, and moved them to different locations on the shelf. It slid open, revealing a doorway and a steep staircase heading down.

"Steel yourself, doctor, and open your mind. Things are only going to get stranger from here." The lord regent cast a flame into his palm. Gaige had seen sorcery firsthand before, but he had seen it done with a catalyst and not with such incredible ease.

"Do you have a hidden catalyst? What spell did you invoke? Or is it a trick? Do you have manganese or phosphorous hidden in your sleeve?"

"So many questions, doctor. What happened to the quest on faith?" The lord regent stared hard at him.

Gaige lifted a hand to adjust his mask, only to find his face bare. There was nowhere to hide.

"My flame feeds from the science of sorcery," the lord regent said and laughed.

And Gaige laughed with him. He decided that, dream or reality, he would find out was going on soon enough. So he followed the red coat with its embroidered wolves and ravens deeper into the ground. They reached a lift made of wood and iron supports. The lord regent gestured Gaige inside and followed, then pulled a lever and the lift began its descent.

When they reached the bottom, Gaige recognized the design of the hall immediately. The stones and the statues: it was the place he had just seen when he touched the pommel of that sword. The place where he had stood at the head of an army and roared for them to go into battle. No dream. He *had* stood here. And that could have no explanation or answer.

"These are the Catacombs of Time, doctor. In these tunnels lived the ones before. They stretch miles in all directions. I have been here for forty years, researching, exploring, and still I have seen only a small part of the whole."

Gaige thought the lord regent looked no more than thirty, so he supposed some of those forty years had been spent perfecting his sorcery.

"Still I have not found all their secrets, likely not even a tenth." The lord regent extended his arms up, and the torches on the walls illuminated. The walls were marked, scrawled with chalk markings, stark white on black. Mathematical equations, alchemical recipes, Brynthian and Fracian scrawlings. Some of the words were even Romarian; more still were alphabets unrecognizable to Gaige.

"In these halls lived an ancient race," said the lord regent. "A race that could cast themselves through time. Sorcery, or science?"

"A bit of both." Gaige smiled a little. The tiny part of him that wanted to argue, to insist that no one could travel through time, was squelched by the part of him that believed, that *knew*.

They continued walking, and the lord regent gave brief

explanations of the symbols on the walls, all his work. Gaige couldn't stop his questions, and some the lord regent even answered. They walked for some time until they reached a crossroads, a tall atrium with a pentagram in the center of the floor. Each triangle of the star was filled with an equation, and in the center of the symbol rested an iron helmet—old, but not anywhere as close to ancient as the artifacts in the hallway with the pillars. The helm had two spiked horns that sprouted horizontally from each side. The eyeholes were circular, similar to those of Gaige's mask.

In front of the helmet was a purple gemstone attached to a necklace. Gaige leaned in and stared at the stone. A maelstrom churned in the center, dark, foreboding, contained by the gem's shell. It called to him, pulled at him not unlike the obsidian sword, but he felt it even deeper in his unbeating heart, as if he knew it, had once owned it, though he knew for certain he had never seen it before. He reached for it.

The lord regent jerked him back.

Gaige took a deep breath. "What am I doing here?" he asked, his voice low, his gaze locked on the stone. He didn't expect the lord regent to answer with truth, and was startled when he did.

"I am far more and far less than the man you see before you. There are powers beyond me, beyond the seekers, beyond the majesty of Brynth." He called up balls of flame in his hands, and the flames spread and grew, licking at his forearms, leaving untouched skin behind. "This is how I began," he said, and the flames snuffed. He gestured at the pentagram. "And this is how you begin, my friend."

"We are friends?" Gaige asked.

"We will be." The lord regent paused. "And we were."

Gaige glanced at the pentagram again, a sliver of premonition weaving through him. "Any other friends I have that I don't know about yet?"

"The girl... the Lycan you saved. And two men, Theron Ward and Kendrick Solomon Kelmoor, also called Kendrick the Cold, though he is far from that."

"Kendrick the Cold? Named after the infamous butcher of Kallibar from three hundred years ago? What parent would saddle their child with such a moniker?"

"You are not looking for someone named after him. You are looking for him. Kendrick. And Theron. And me. My younger self."

Gaige waited for the surprise, the shock, the denial that should come at such an assertion. There was none. There was only acknowledgment of the truth. It defied logic. It defied science. It even defied sorcery. And yet he did not doubt the lord regent's words.

"You don't look surprised."

"Why should I be surprised? You're sending a dead man you reanimated at your dining room table to find two men who died three centuries ago and a third man who never died and stands before me now. What could make more sense?"

The lord regent threw back his head and laughed.

"Why do you not go to do this yourself?" Gaige asked.

"There are many reasons, but I will explain the ones your mind will allow you to understand. I cannot risk encountering my younger self. And more than that, if I carry myself three centuries into the past, to a time where I was young and green, my current level of power will be recognized by our enemies. They will be alerted. They will move too quickly."

"*Our* enemies?"

"Leviathan," said the lord regent. "A name you will come to know."

Gaige nodded. "If I find them... these friends I do not know—"

"When you find them," the lord regent corrected.

"When I find them," Gaige said, "how do I convince them that what I say is true? How do I convince them that I know you?"

"Tell Theron that I killed my first rat in the dungeons beneath Norburg and followed behind him as he dragged Ken on a sledge toward Wardbrook. Tell Ken that his whole life he meant good, and that does count. It counts. Love matters. Tell them both that my first and only love had hair of spun gold and enough skill and muscle to land any soldier on his back. Tell them that. They will believe you."

The lord regent held his arm out toward the pentagram in invitation, and from his belt he drew a long knife of gleaming gold and steel, the hilt engraved with intricate runes.

A preternatural calm settled over him as Gaige stepped into the pentagram, one foot on either side of the helmet that sat on the ground. As he moved, he felt no pain, and he could not say he missed his ruined, twisted limb. Perhaps being dead was not so bad after all.

"Pick up the necklace," the lord regent said, gesturing with the tip of the dagger. "It will be your only way back to the here and now in the catacombs of time."

Gaige did as he instructed, again feeling the pull of the gem. He slid the thick chain over his neck, the gem hanging at his sternum. The storm within the amethyst depths swirled and roiled.

The lord regent held out his arm and made a shallow cut across his palm, then turned his hand as he pumped his fist so his blood fell drop by drop onto the helmet. He spoke in tongues. Gaige thought that if he still possessed a heart that could beat, it would be slamming against his ribs right now. A purple mist began to rise from the chalk lines of the pentagram. The lord regent dropped to kneel and slammed his bleeding palm to the ground directly before the helmet. The purple mist converged above him and a black orb hovered in the air above, shiny and sleek.

Turning. Turning.

Images began to take form in the center of the orb. A forest in late spring. A waterfall. An unkindness of ravens in a stark, dead tree.

The orb expanded and Gaige could not look away. There was fear, yes. But what was fear to a dead man? Excitement surged. Here was what he had searched for his entire life. Here were the answers of the beyond.

Noise accosted him, the rushing water cascading over rock, tumbling to the river below so loud he could hear nothing else.

The image of the lord regent was fading.

"Repeat their names." The lord regent's voice was faint and far away.

"Theron Ward," Gaige yelled. "Kendrick Solomon Kelmoor." Then: "Your name? I need your name."

The roar was so loud now that Gaige thought his ears bled.

He heard nothing, and then, so faint he thought the voice came from a million miles away: "I am Aldous Weaver."

But somehow, he already knew that, before he heard the words.

End

If you enjoy Catacombs of Time **please leave an online review** to help other readers decide on this book.

Read book 3—The Pyres—now!

Keep reading for a sample of the next book in the Sword and Sorcery Series…***The Pyres***!

BONUS SAMPLE CHAPTER

THE PYRES

The one eyed man—Theron Ward thought of himself that way now—dipped his throbbing, bloodied fists into the bowl of solid gold on the slender marble altar before him. The water lapped up the crimson from his knuckles and the bowl darkened, intensified in its opacity, the silver Romarian sovereign at the bottom becoming harder to see. He smiled. He would keep at this until he could see nothing in the bowl but his reflection against a surface like crimson glass.

He looked up, listened to the chirping of the birds. It was a beautiful morning…well, it would have been if he were still Theron Ward, going for a walk in the garden with some maiden. Which he would have been.

Three years, to be exact.

It had been a spring morning just like this when he had walked with a lady, Mildrith, through the garden of his estate, Wardbrook, in the green countryside of Brynth with its rolling hills… *And Mildrith's rolling hills, or was it Lady Caitlyn who had those perfect pale…* It did not feel like three years past, more like thirty with all that had taken place. All the carnage. Enough bloodshed for the lifetimes of ten men to call themselves seasoned, and he knew his journey had hardly begun. It was painful knowledge to bear.

"Some wine," he said.

Promptly a cup was filled on a table that stood off to the left of the tiled courtyard, a jeweled cup, made of solid gold. It was lustrous in its shining density—*lustrous like the tanned breasts of the serving wench who filled it...*

He was drunk and melancholy, lonely for a woman, and, for a moment, he thought he was back there, in his garden with Mildrith, or Caitlyn or whoever.

"Focus on the fight, not the maid's tits," said Olav Yegarov from the sideline.

"I'll focus on what I please, Yegarov," Theron said without turning to the man and still focusing on the girl. He smiled at her the way he had smiled at the young lady in the carriage on the road that morning as they had ridden into Chech. It was the smile he always used with the fairer sex. It had been perfect once.

The girl brought the wine over, looking at the floor as she did.

Not long ago she would have been weak in the knees at the sight of him. She would have dreamt of him in the night, in the best way. He had been handsome. He had been a lord and had a name that was honored. He had once believed himself a hero, a warrior with an ambition for righteousness, a leader who was loved by many.

That was a different time.

Since Dentin, the once handsome smile now made women scowl and turn away. The maid looked over his bare torso a moment, then up at his face, and she winced. In fear, pity, disgust—he did not think long on it, but he too looked away and was blushing just as she was, regretting that he had smiled at all.

Some gentleman I am. A proper fucking hero.

He felt older than his years as he watched the girl go. His ambitions had become nothing more than surviving through the winter, and now that the task was done and the flowers were in bloom, he did not feel accomplishment. He did not feel reborn. Only more exhausted than he had been in the fall.

Being Olav's escort was supposed to be easy money, simple tasks of collection, limited violence. A chance to pool resources and move on to larger things. Perhaps a lodge of hunters.

It had been anything but simple. The violence seemed to have no limits, and the resources that had been promised had not materialized.

Theron looked up as the next brute walked into the square of white stone tiles, his feet planted in the blood that Theron had beaten out of his first opponent, the opponent who was still twitching as a barber-surgeon shook his head at the pulverized form at his feet.

"Next to step forth in place of Baron Kvorag, of the fiefdom of Chech of the vast country of Romaria, is Timmut, son of Timmut," announced the caller. "And who stands for you, Sir Olav Yegarov?"

"One-Eye remains my champion," said Olav as he waved one of his spidery hands toward Theron. Olav Yegarov was a tall, hollow-faced man, sharp features above a square jaw, his straight white hair cropped tight to his scalp. His face was always clean-shaven. No matter how long they had been on the road, a sharp razor was always part of his morning ritual. Lately, Theron caught himself watching Yegarov shave, and thinking about slitting the man's throat for all he had put them through. But Theron's word was his word, and his choices were his own, and so he completed the tasks asked of him for the coin he asked of Yegarov.

"Very well," said the caller. He stepped into the center of the square.

This Timmut, son of Timmut, was a large man, a barbarian, a warrior of the Steppe. His hair and beard were long, straight, and black, his eyes narrow and cruel. It did not matter. Theron Ward would fight two.

"Wait." Theron's voice came out in a low rasp. He had been drinking too much and puffing on his medicine pipe too frequently as of late. Last night had been no exception. "Two. Give me two. So we can get this done faster."

"Theron, are you—" came the beginnings of a remonstration from the red-hooded young man to Olav's left: Aldous Weaver, heretic monk turned sorcerer, monster hunter, younger brother, student, target for verbal assault, and good friend. Aldous clung to the intricately carved wooden staff in his right hand as though it would anchor him in a storm. Which, in fact, it would.

"Two," Theron said.

There was a grunt that may have been laughter from the monstrosity of a human being to Olav's right, a man who should have been the one pounding apart faces with his fists, but he was not permitted to partake in the contest because of the fact that one of his hands was made of iron. Kendrick the Cold. He was a little leaner and a little bit uglier, with his head shaved to the scalp and a thick, braided brown beard coming down from his scarred chin, sporting a bone from the left hand of the Emerald Witch that Theron had brought back as a gift. Ken's always scrutinizing, beady eyes stared from the shadows set by his primitive brow, peering now past Theron to gaze at the second man who was stepping from the green lawn into the breaking square.

Theron turned to face his opponents. He had thought he was past moral ambiguity... *I had a code.* He looked over at the man on the ground, who finally stopped twitching. He looked at his fists. Battered. So battered they'd be nearly useless, so he'd need to get creative with the two now in the square. He'd have time to feel guilty and add a few more skeletons to his closet of never-spoken regrets when the task was done.

So with resolve to finish the evil thing, this mercenary act of—with his bare fists—bloodying poor men on behalf of rich men, Theron advanced toward his foes: Timmut and the second man, Red Rolph, a beast from the northern isles, a place separated from Romaria's most northern point by a week or so on the fastest ships in the best of weather. The northerner was thin and wiry, exceptionally so, though he was tall and his arms were long, with large, bony fists at the ends. His hair was wild and knotted like his beard, and his skin was tattooed with blue rune markings.

He will fight to the death.

Theron had met many such men during his time in the isles.

Theron took the golden bowl from the altar and placed it at the foot of the marble formation.

"Begin," cried the caller.

Timmut moved left to begin circling to Theron's flank.

Theron sprang at the easterner first. Engaging him in a grapple, he pulled himself close, chest to chest with his foe, wrapping him tight with the strength of a bear.

The northerner was right there, his fist coming in a wide, powerful—if poorly aimed—hook. Theron twisted his core as he held on to the struggling Timmut and thrust the fat warrior into the other fighter's fist headfirst. The northerner threw another blow as Theron shoved away the stunned Timmut, and ducked under the wide strike. He pressed forward, wrapping the northman round the waist and lifting him from the ground. He squeezed with all the vigor he could muster, forcing the air from the northerner right before he twisted him around and smashed him shoulder first into the white marble tile. The snap of bone echoed through the courtyard, followed by a scream and the fluttering of wings as the nearby birds took flight.

Theron caught a glimpse of the serving girl's pale face, wide eyes, and open mouth. He was willing to wager she hadn't enjoyed witnessing that either.

Releasing the writhing northerner, Theron turned to face Timmut, who came barreling at him. Theron had enough time to see him—he had enough time to know how he *would have* gotten out of the way—but he did not have the time to follow through. Timmut went low, his shoulder dropped, flesh and muscle clapping as he smashed into Theron's abdominal wall.

He wrapped his arm around Timmut's head, and then he felt his feet leave the ground.

The world was still to Theron's eye. His mind slowed, and the flapping of the bird's wings and chirping sounded far off, as did the pained groans of the northerner.

The yelling of Kendrick, Aldous, and Yegarov was all so far away.

Theron saw his own filthy golden hair swaying before him as they went down, those few dreadful feet to that cursed, slippery white marble floor, to the floor of the breaking square.

He admired the surface—*the sensuality of its violence, smooth and cold like damp silk, but dare you crash upon it*—

The pain was there before he heard the slap of his upper back followed by the sickening knock of the back of his skull—

—*you will shatter*—

—colliding with that most murderous of floors.

As fast as it came, the pain was gone.

Darkness. Lightning, a shower of lightning, purple veins of it shredding through the blackness. Oceans of blood, drums, and the faraway sound of wind whistling through a chime.

Nothing.

He could not feel just then, nor could he hear but for the silent resonance that rings through a skull when it is thumped upon an unforgiving surface. But he could see. He stared with great contempt at the golden bowl that he had placed upon the ground, at the murky mix of blood and water and, drowned at the bottom, the silver Romarian sovereign.

Then all at once his head throbbed and he heard the mad screams of the small audience to the spectacle.

"Get up, One-Eye. Get up, you Brynthian mongrel scum!" Yegarov roared in common speech.

"Stay focused, Ward. Stay focused and roll him over," Kendrick said calmly, and Theron focused on his words above Yegarov's and the foreign barking of Baron Kvorag.

Timmut's head was still locked in Theron's hold when they had hit the ground, and so he, too, had felt the hard lesson of the marble. But he felt it much harder. Theron was first to gain his faculties, but the northerner with the devastated shoulder was getting back to his feet as he fought through the pain. Theron needed to finish Timmut.

"Like a snake to a rabbit, Ward. Like a fucking snake to a rabbit," Kendrick said in a voice just above a hush, faded beneath the other sounds, but Theron heard it.

Like a snake to a rabbit.

His grip round the easterner's head had loosened from the impact of the takedown, but now Theron tightened his hold as he wrapped his legs around Timmut's waist and, tensing like some jungle constrictor, he pulled and rotated with a deranged fury.

Timmut's jaw snapped.

"There it is." Ken's voice.

Theron would have let it end there, but Timmut pulled a sharpened stone from his waist, adding a weapon to a weaponless fight. He slashed blindly at Theron's throat. Theron kept his hold on Timmut's throat and blocked the man's thrust with his free hand.

This was no longer a fight to victory; it was a fight to the death.

"Finish it!" Yegarov said.

The edge of the makeshift blade kissed Theron's skin.

"Kill him!" Aldous's voice shattered, as it was still in the habit of doing, and the words came out like the shrill scream of a mad banshee, and it was this that spurred Theron most. He tightened his hold.

The easterner gurgled a moment and then his neck snapped and he went silent and still. *Like a snake to a rabbit.*

Theron rolled the twitching mass from his body and narrowly evaded a straight kick from the northerner. He sprang to his feet, and made some distance between himself and his crippled foe.

Why are you here? the child in Theron wanted to ask the wounded barbarian that he faced, for they had no true quarrel.

For what do you fight? the philosopher in him wanted to ask.

The northerner roared like a bear, his oak eyes gleaming with frenzy, his mane of wild, knotted brown hair sweeping side to side as he came steadily forth to his obliteration.

Admirable.

Theron took an unexpected jab to his face from the spear-like arm of his lanky foe, and his already unstable vision momentarily intensified in its obstruction. A second jab he avoided on instinct, and Theron slipped low and to the left, coming in with his right fist as he did, thudding it hard into the northerner's ribs. The man caved forward and

Theron gripped the knotted hair, pulled down, and leaned back as he plunged his knee outward and up into the northerner's face. It made a crunching noise as the teeth shattered.

Fill the bowl. That is how this works. When you can no longer see the coin at the bottom, we win the contest, and I get what is mine without further bloodshed. Theron told himself that was a good reason to do something, to prevent *further bloodshed*.

His head was ringing as he manhandled the northerner to the altar, both hands locked firmly in the mane of matted hair. He kicked him in the backs of the knees, crumbling the mercenary into a position of prayer above the golden bowl.

Theron split that stranger's skull apart with a crack against the edge of the altar. There came the sucking of air when the connecting plates of bone fragmented, split, and caved, and then the brain and its encasing fluid dripped out like the white and yolk of a cracked egg. The blood and pinkish-gray chunks of brain lathered in crimson ran down the edge of the stone and filled the bowl until the contents flooded over the rim and formed red rivers in the crevices between the tiles.

He dropped the corpse and looked down; peering back at him through the gold-rimmed mirror of crimson glass was the face of a man he did not want to know, a scowling, wounded beast with a pain in his heart that would not cease.

I am done, done with this.

"I am no mercenary," he said.

He put a hand on the back of his head, and then looked at his fingers. *No blood,* but it bloody ached.

A heavy hand landed on his shoulder and he turned to face Kendrick. "Interesting tactic, hunter, using the back of your skull like that to break your fall. I wouldn't recommend overplaying it, though," Ken said, his face void of expression.

"Tonight when we reach Brasov we part ways with

Olav, that…gremlin," Theron said, and peered over Ken's massive shoulder to see Olav walking toward Baron Kvorag.

"And get back to what we said we'd do back in Brynth, after Dentin?" Ken asked.

There was no remonstration in Ken's tone, but Theron felt it anyway.

"Yes, back to our oaths, back to killing beasts." Theron turned his head to the pulverized corpses; they looked almost as if a monster had at them. "I fear when the excitement settles, when we move on from here, these events will have further darkened me."

"I fear they will have darkened us all," Aldous said, as he approached. He pulled his red hood low, as though he wanted to avoid looking at the mess. Which was fair, Theron thought, because Aldous had seen a good deal in his eighteen years, and the fact that he was not immune to the sight of violence was only a good mark on the boy's character. When he had screamed the words "kill him" earlier it had not been out of bloodlust, only fear for Theron and a desire to see the thing done and over with.

"So…when I write about the events that transpired here, in this chapter of Theron Ward's legend, what do I write?" Aldous asked. The boy's tone did hold remonstration, and once again, Theron felt it.

"You write the truth. You write what you saw. Remember your father's words. *An honest writer is the most virtuous of heroes—*" Theron began.

"*One who lies is the most deplorable of all villains,*" Aldous finished.

The sound of arguing in the Romarian tongue, which Theron was learned in, caused him to turn from the conversation with his companions. His employer, or as Theron described him, *his client*, Olav Yegarov, stood in the bloodied square where the dispute was supposed to have just come to an end.

But it appeared that here in Romaria, the men in power were the same lying, thieving, bastard slavers as the high and mighty of Brynth. And as he often did when in the company of titled men, Theron wondered what made a beast, what a monster? Was it claws and fur matted with blood? Long fangs and slithering tongues? Tails and wings, horns and scales... *Or is it all in the eyes? When the glint of life and passion is gone, and all that remains are dead orbs drunk with the blood and tears of all those they have broken on a whim.*

"Yegarov, what is that old shit spouting from his comfy chair, in his cozy blankets?" asked Kendrick. The big man had been holding Theron's claymore in its sheath, and he handed it to Theron.

The hefty blade felt heavier than its usual seven pounds after the exertion of the unarmed combat.

"Kvorag is claiming it was an unfair contest," said Yegarov in the common tongue.

"Of course it was unfair. Theron just fought two men and won...with one eye." It was Aldous who spoke now. He pulled back his hood. Theron often marveled at how quickly the boy had grown in height and bone structure despite the hardships of the road. Perhaps he was only late to grow and would not forever be paltry. But it was not just the boy's appearance that had aged; it was his demeanor, his essence that had grown the most. When Theron met him, nearly two years past, he had been a nervous, volatile whelp. Now he was a calm, fierce, wolfish man who controlled fire...*sometimes.*

Other times he was still a volatile whelp...who failed to control fire.

"He is not talking about this contest," Yegarov began. "He is referring to the contest, the horse race, where he first developed this sizeable debt to me." Yegarov was smiling. This seemed to be a trend in the claims of his debtors. They were all cheated at gambling, all wealthy, all of some status, all refusing to pay.

None of them were good men, or good women, but collecting debts from them for a cheater and swindler was not about right or wrong.

"Yegarov, had I known the extent of how wretched a man you were prior to our contract, I would have never followed through," said Theron.

"And here I was thinking you and I, and Ken and Aldous, had developed everlasting friendships. You wound me, Theron…but our contract ends tonight. When the sun goes down we may finally part ways in Brasov… But before that, convince this old man that it is in his best interest to pay what is owed."

Theron spat, and pulled the claymore free from the sheath. The great sword had been many times modified over the past nine years, but it was still the same sword, the same parting gift from his father before Theron began the hunt. As it had been all those years ago, it was the tool of his art, and with it he had painted red on scenes of snow and ice, forests, swamps, manors, and hovels, and the decks of ships at sea. Nine years and here he was, with the same sword on a killing path.

On the spring lawn, five boys as green as the grass stood, hands on sword hilts as they surrounded their baron. They were not the hard men; the hard men were the slaves Theron had just beaten to death. These were the pretty young boys the baron liked to keep around to look at, to live through vicariously. Not one them had a beard, faces like babes.

Theron was capable of killing them all before Baron Kvorag's piss finished running down his leg. He didn't want to do that, not in the least, but with his one eye he stared at the boys like there was nothing in the whole world he wanted to do more than yell in bloody joy as he hacked them screaming limb from limb. He always had a hard stare, not as hard as Ken's, though, who was standing next to him giving the boys the same look, but worse. No thrill in it, nothing in it at all but the promise that death was so very close, so very real, and so very unstoppable.

"Tell them to walk away, to find a new master," said Aldous as he walked into the square, so now all four of them stood on the ground bloodied by the baron's defeat. A ball of flame ignited and hovered an inch or so above the intricately carved staff that Aldous held in his right hand. The young bodyguards gasped at the sight. If they were not already broken by the looks of Theron and Ken, they had no fight in them now.

"If they fight us, they will die. If they don't, after we leave, Kvorag will have them killed. Tell them that Yegarov," Ken said.

Yegarov spoke in Romarian. His voice was calm, pleading almost.

The young men remained, and for a moment it looked as if they would defend the old wretch. Theron took a single step forward, his sword over his shoulder. They did not move forward or back, but their swords lowered a few inches.

Ken stepped forward, and Aldous as well, the wizard moving to the front, the ball of flame above his staff growing as he raised his other hand to it and whispered to the fire, words the others could not hear. The flame twisted and bent into a wing, then a talon, and a snapping maw of a wolf.

The swords went all the way down, and the boys did not speak as they orchestrated their retreat. The baron yelled and shook his gold- and gem-encrusted cane as his would-be guards gathered their things from the lawn and prepared to abandon their lord. Kvorag finally stood when he saw one of the young men taking a bottle of wine from the grass. He tossed his blankets to the floor, and on old, brittle knees he stumbled at the young man and tried to wrestle the bottle of wine away.

Likely Yegarov was not the only man Kvorag owed. With the civil war raging across the country at its peaking point of violence, these were desperate times. The young men were trying to take anything they could before setting off into dangerous country to find another lecherous old man to live off. Or perhaps they'd join the Dog Eater and his ragtag army and begin burning small towns and raping women and beheading children in their chapels. The options were limited in this country for those who were intent on a life free of conflict.

The boy shoved Kvorag to the ground, made off with the bottle, mounted his horse, and rode off with the rest. The baron crawled after him a short distance, then collapsed entirely and wept.

~

In the end they collected what was owed. They took a horse and a cart, and on it a chest filled with the last bit of a broken baron's gold.

"Where will you go now?" Yegarov asked, after they had ridden for a few miles down a wide road surrounded by rocky ravines and thick green woodland.

"We will escort you to Brasov, as agreed. We should make it there with at least an hour, maybe more, before sundown. You will pay us, and we will go our separate ways," Theron said. He was about to say more, but before he did he saw signs of combat on the road. When he turned to Kendrick and the man gave him a cold nod, it was clear he saw the same.

Upturned dirt, boots pushed through mud, smears where bodies fell, faded red where they were dragged off. Torn blue fabric; from a dress, perhaps? The lady in the carriage on the road this very morn had worn a dress of this exact shade.

"Likely ambushed that same convoy we saw this morning." Ken said what Theron was thinking.

He was about to respond when he caught the smell. It was faint, for all around them life and spring bloomed on the trees and vines, colorful flower buds bursting open, spreading wide in the season of birth. It was not enough, though, to cover the scent of death, and of the beast that followed.

"Ach! What is that smell?" Yegarov asked.

"What I've been waiting for," Theron answered.

Read The Pyres now!

Keep reading for a FREE bonus short story—*I Remember My First Time*!

BONUS FREE SHORT STORY

I REMEMBER MY FIRST TIME

On the seventh evening of the chase, the Brynthian hulk caught us beneath a blazing red sun drowning in the endless sea. They had more men, more guns, and a goodly dose of arrogance—that alone was enough to sink us. And the two other destroyers several leagues behind, well, they were just a bloody formality. That was what they thought, the king's bloodhounds on the sea, those bastards who were hunting us.

But they had never faced *us*.

They had never faced the *Sea Maggot* and her reinforced brass hull. They had never gotten close enough to board, to suffer the eagle accuracy of our muskets and pistols. They had never seen the flash of steel wielded by hands from a score of different nations, steel thirsty for the blood of the Brynthian Empire, the blood of those mage-killing, temple-smashing, book-burning tyrants.

They had never faced our mage, Stiggis the Walker.

He was old as a man could get without being a corpse. His filthy white beard was closer to yellow, and closer still to brown where he braided it through golden rings. His cheeks were sunken deep into his skull and his eyes were grey and filmy like a blind man's, but even so, Stiggis had sight better than any man I'd ever known. Despite his gauntness and apparent age, he was so tall and wide in frame that it was hard to find a horse that could carry him, hence the moniker "the Walker." He was called a druid in his homeland, a bender of the elements. He said he spoke to spirits, in the air and the sea, and I believed him. I had seen him do it many times, and each time the hair on my neck would stand on end and gooseflesh would rise.

Stiggis was a danger to any ship that did battle with us. I'd once seen him summon an undertow so strong it pulled three launches filled with men into water that had been calm as glass only moments before. He kept a maelstrom whirling and killed every last man, and he did it sitting in a tree on the shore.

But our greatest asset still was our captain, and it was she and she alone who saw us through those terrible days that came after our night facing the Brynthian hulk.

The enemy ship was in firing range, and even though I knew the plan, I knew the cost too, and I do confess that my hands were shaking like they used to every time I saw Hilda in the Church of the Luminescent as a lad. I was filled with a mixture of anticipation and excitement, but also an unshakable fear that the thing I was looking at was going to destroy me.

They were two hundred and fifty yards to our port side, half their ship behind our stern, but that didn't matter, for the Brynthian hulk towered with eighty-four guns. Even getting hit by a portion of their broadside would be catastrophic.

Our captain stood dead center of the deck, smiling a sharp white grin that glowed in contrast to her dark brown skin. She wore the pink and white scars that embroidered the flesh of her arms, face, and shaved head with pride, testament to a hundred battles at sea, on land, waist deep in a bloody tide on a white sandy beach. She fought for those scars.

She had sailed as first mate under Filthy Jack Lawrence. She had beaten Stiggis the Walker at his own game of wits on a wager, and won our crew his services and, later, his loyalty. She met Admiral Wallace on the high sea, gave him a thrashing, invited him to tea, and that night he joined her crew. We call him Wayward Wallace now.

Given enough time, she was a woman capable of swaying anyone to her cause. And it wasn't always with a sharp sword that she did so, but a sharp tongue and a sharp mind as needs must. She was an ordinary mortal, not a drop of magic in her blood, a dark-skinned woman, by her own words a pagan in a pig-skinned man's world, where the Church of the Luminescent ruled, and their beast the Leviathan Company reached its tentacles out from the abyss to take whatever and whomever it pleased. Against these odds she had resisted and done so admirably. To a man, we idolized her. She was more than our captain; she was our will to fight.

She swayed us to her impossible plan with a few precise sentences. Now, she brought us closer to the Brynthian hulk with its three levels of guns, a volley being loaded. We did not try to gain speed, or load quicker and fire before they did. Instead, the captain ordered Krigs to turn us hard at them. Right at them.

I stared at the dark mouths of the cannons and was certain that when that volley was unleashed we would be done for, and so I am not ashamed to admit—for these were still the early years of my career as Timothy "Golden Boy" O'Connor. I was yet to hang a prince and yet to flay a sultan. I was yet to ever even have killed a man in sword combat—my legs were shaking as well as my hands, and my balls felt like beetles trying to squirm back into my stomach and scuttle out my ass.

But I trusted the captain's plan, I trusted my mates, and I trusted the primordial power of Stiggis the Walker to see us through. The wizard was standing in the center of the deck next to the captain, the top of her head hardly past his waist, his primitive long axe in hand as he began to speak to the spirits. It was a chant in an ancient tongue that started as a whisper and slowly grew. And as his chant reached toward the sky, we steeled ourselves for what was to come.

The wood of the deck beneath his feet came alive, peeling back in thin strands that first twirled and knotted together, then split into thick, branchlike forms that wrapped round the wizard's legs, grounding him sturdy as a tree. With a strong grip on his coat, the captain braced herself, and I clung to one of the rope railings, of which we had many on the ship, for sailing on the *Sea Maggot* was sailing rough, and fighting rougher still. Of all the formidable skills I honed in my years on that deck, an iron grip was the first.

"Now, Stiggis!" cried the captain as she peered through her telescope.

To a man, we stood, cutlasses and pistols drawn, the air pulled from our very lungs as Stiggis drew his magic from the air, the wind, the sea.

The wizard clenched his fist at his side. His veins bulged in his neck and his chant became the sounds of madness as he roared with such volume it contested the boom of the admiral's cannons as they fired. Great metal balls hurtled toward us at incredible speed, but not too fast to see, just too fast for us to avoid. That was likely what they thought.

The crew knew otherwise. We had seen Stiggis do magic before. We had seen the effect of magic's delicate economy on his form, for after the spell was cast, there was always a cost. The greater the spell, the closer to death Stiggis walked.

And the spell he wove now was the greatest.

Before we were sent to a watery grave, the ship tilted hard to its starboard side, sending the crew scuttling across the deck, clutching for anything that was tied down. The sea grew beneath us in a monstrous wave so tall that all three levels of guns were evaded, their projectiles smashing into the wall of water we now rode.

"Brace!" the captain ordered, and the grin on her face stretched ear to ear as she squinted against the mist spraying up from the sea.

The ship sat atop the crest of the wave. My stomach was in my chest, and then we dropped like a wagon racing down a treacherously steep hill and my gut dropped at the same time as my breakfast rose. The prow raced down toward the enemy deck, men like ants scurrying fore and aft.

The moment our figurehead—a woman's form, bare from the waist up, her features twisted and decayed, with maggots crawling from between her lips—crashed into their starboard, sending splinters of wood in every direction, my shoulders jarred and my grip was torn from the rope. I went sprawling and hit my head hard on the deck, and when I got to my feet my vision was obscured with crimson. My ears rang as men screamed and muskets blared. I wiped the blood from my eyes, stumbling, bile in the back of my throat, seeing everything through a hazy lens. I could hardly stand. The musket ball that ripped into the muscle of my shoulder assisted me in lying back down.

I vaguely recall dragging myself across the deck unashamedly screaming in agony, tears running down my face, but the memory of Stiggis falling to one knee wearing the face of death is not vague at all.

A swarm of purple—legs and arms and faces twisted with hate, sabers and boarding axes, pistols and muskets—clambered onto the deck. I remained still on the ground, my shoulder heavy and weak at the same time, with a throb that beat in tandem with the combat around me. I was in no condition to fight. I was not the best fighter when in condition for it. I decided to play dead, until one of the purple coats stabbed me in the arse cheek. When I squealed like a pig, he pulled the blade free and I rolled over just in time to stare down the barrel of his musket.

He pulled the trigger.

Misfire.

I laughed, and years later I came to think that Timothy "Golden Boy" O'Connor became a man that day.

He raised his musket like a spear, but before he could stick me through, Wayward Wallace charged across the deck and his wooden club whistled through the air and cracked against the purple coat's skull. Instead of my guts on the deck, it was bits of his brain raining down on me in a shower.

I wiped brain and blood from my eyes and saw the captain fighting five men with her two Kheldeshi blades.

"Up, Golden Boy!" Wallace shouted, and he hoisted me up to my feet, then spun round to parry a saber. In two blows—one to the side of the knee, the other to the throat when the man fell—Wallace slew another. I heard the report of a rifle—it had a sharper crack than a musket—and then Wallace went down.

I grabbed him and dragged him toward the stern, passing Stiggis, who had not moved from the place he had collapsed, but from his lips came the sound of a low hum, words without form in a tongue I did not know, and again I felt my lungs tighten, the air thin. Somehow, Stiggis was rallying the forces to him, and before my eyes, he seemed to fill with life.

He surged to his feet and, with a roar, axe in hand, charged at the Brynthian hulk. Our prow was buried deep in her starboard, grappling hooks holding us close despite the raging waves beneath the ships. The wizard climbed onto their deck and drew a deep breath. Arms back and out to the sides, neck straining forward, he breathed out like one of the winged, scaled beasts his ancestors worshipped. Each man his breath touched turned to a statue of ice, features twisted in a mask of horror. Then he swept his axe back and forth, hewing down men left and right. But his blade did not cut. Instead the frozen men shattered.

"Cut her loose!" Stiggis cried, and he took a volley of musket fire. He was still swinging his axe, and chanting his spells, blood pouring from his mouth as purple-coated men swarmed him.

"Get us underway!" the captain cried to the helmsman, and then she unloaded her pistol into the face of a man not three feet from her.

"What about Stiggis?" I yelled. He was too important a man to leave behind. And he was my friend.

"This is his will, to die with his axe in his hand!" said Wallace. "Has he not told us so many a time?"

I looked to the captain and then to Stiggis, and as I did, he brought his massive axe down, severing one of the ropes that bound the two ships.

His sacrifice and commitment inspired me beyond any way I can explain, and I found a sword sticking out of a dead man's chest, its hilt wet with blood, and cut at the ropes of the grappling hooks that tethered us to our foe. Next to me, Wallace was back on his feet. His ear was gone and half his head was covered in blood, and when he saw me sawing at the ropes he smiled at me, pulled his knife from his belt, and did the same.

I caught a glimpse of the captain, a whirlwind of death, clearing the remaining enemy from our deck. Across the increasing gap between the ships, she and Stiggis stared at each other for what felt like a long moment. Then Stiggis nodded.

The wind took our sails and drew us away. We all watched as a maelstrom began to form, and as it grew, it pulled the enemy ship in toward its center. Frantic, the purple coats climbed the rigging, spun the wheel, pulled on ropes, and finally cut them. To no avail.

On the deck, Stiggis was pushed back until he was pressed against the rail, still swinging his axe. And then he was pushed overboard into the gaping maw of the maelstrom. Tears welled in my eyes for the sacrifice of that legendary warrior.

We sailed away while their ship followed Stiggis into the depths.

It was another day still before we reached our wharf. We were separated now from the remaining Brynthian destroyers by near ten hours. But we had little doubt they knew where we were heading and they would follow. We had no time to dally, no opportunity to lick our wounds.

We anchored the *Sea Maggot*, and I recall how empty our launches looked as we passed between the natural stone walls of the cove that towered into the sky. We had wrapped our dead and sent them over the side as we fled the destroyers. Now, I stared up at the stalactites and listened to the oars. The last time our oars echoed as they dipped into this water, paddling us toward the fort, we had twenty-two more men packed into the launches, men I had called friends. They would be mourned, but first they would be avenged.

Wayward Wallace helped me up the beach, though he was as injured as I.

"You're all right, Golden Boy," Wallace said, with six inches of wooden splinter sticking out of the monstrous muscles on the back of his neck. "Just brush it off. We'll have a drink in the fort and take that hot piece of lead right out of your shoulder." He slapped me on the side of my arse that wasn't bleeding. "And sew up your new asshole tight as it were before."

I was shaking from the pain and sweating profusely, but when we reached the fort in the cave, the fort that we called home, I felt a rise in my vigor, if only for long enough to get to the rum. Wallace no doubt felt the same, because all at once the two of us, propping each other up, stumbled as quickly as we could through the front gate.

An hour and a jug of rum later, I was drunk—thank the forces that be for that—when our medic, Shakes, dug the lead ball out of my shoulder. We didn't have the time to stitch up every man's wounds, so he used a hot iron. I screamed and tears rolled down my cheeks, but I thanked him when it was done. And hoped that the stink was only burning flesh and that I had not finally lost the fight against my bowels.

I was still drinking—I suppose I should not have been—when I heard whistles and snare drums on the beach. The purple coats were amassing. I limped across the floor to where our men sharpened their blades and cleaned the barrels of their guns. Their faces were grim.

The captain strode among the men, assigning tasks. She sent me to carry a crate of small glass globes filled with oil, slow-burning rope wicks at the mouth of each, to Wallace, who had been assigned to one of the fort's two defensive towers. They were cylindrical and perfectly smooth outside and in, smooth as wet stone, the walls a foot thick, with narrow slits for firing at the enemy. What tools had been used to make the fort thousands of years ago was a complete mystery. The natives of the island we called home, Poino, believed it once belonged to the gods, and so they never dared set foot here. Now it belonged to devils.

With my shoulder screaming, I hobbled up the stairs. Wallace's wounds were bandaged, his barrel chest bare, a half-full bottle of rum in his hand, and he looked lovingly down at the Deck Sweeper, his five barreled musket. Laid out neatly next to him were eight more muskets, all loaded.

"I have killing on my mind," Wallace said with a big smile. "Let's make Stiggis proud."

I nodded and set down the crate. A diamond skink scuttled across the worn stone floor on its eight scaled legs, and as it went, all I could think about was how I had gone from being on a ship bound for the seminary in Fracia four years ago, where I was set to become a priest in the Church of the Luminescent, to being part of a pirate crew, to sitting here in this fortress looking at a lizard scuttle across the ground, just as we had scuttled to our hiding place. Wallace saw it too, and cracked his foot down on its skull in a flash.

It crunched.

I cringed.

I didn't have the stomach for cruelty. I saw violence all the time; I was a gentleman of fortune, after all and fortune's path was a fucking bloody one. I loaded cannons, sure. I fired a pistol and a musket onto the enemy deck, threw a lit glass globe and plugged my ears as I heard men screaming, burning alive. But for those first four years, with charm and wit, with excuses and evasive tactics, I had avoided being thrust into the thick of a close-quarters combat. This battle at sea was the most direct fight I had been in since joining the crew. Usually the captain's name ensured that we faced paltry resistance when taking our prizes. I thought our luck had to end eventually.

I looked out a firing hole down the beach at the purple coats gathering there. Admiral "Gallows" Gareth was there with them, a short, angry man, wearing a black tricorn hat and flowing purple cloak. His chin was up, that proud bastard on his high horse. Literally. He rode his white mare in on one of the launches.

I turned from the firing hole and stared at the crushed lizard. "Why'd you do that?"

"Why'd I do what?" Wallace asked. He kicked the dead lizard over, leaned back against the wall, closed his eyes, then took a swig of his rum. "Crunch that lizard there like that?" Wallace smiled and ran a hand through his greasy blond hair, and with his other hand he put down his rum and began tying a pigtail.

"That is why we call you Golden Boy, Tim. That is why we call you Golden Boy," Wallace said, and then tied his other pigtail and relaxed his head back against the stone wall. "Pass me my pipe and a match, would you? The bowl's already packed."

I went to his coat that he had shed and tossed in the corner, retrieved the pipe from the inner breast pocket where he always kept it, and brought it to him.

"Sit down," he said. "Have a drink, have a smoke."

"You are the kindest cruel man I have ever met, good Wallace. I would appreciate a puff of your fine leaves if you'd allow it." I placed my back to the wall and slid down so that Wallace and I were shoulder to shoulder. He lit the pipe and took a healthy pull, then passed it to me and I did the same. Wallace was the man to go to when it came to smoking well, for he knew a thing or two about herbs, and he had collected plants from the world round during his journeys on the *Sea Maggot*. He kept some in pots that the captain allowed him to keep in her cabin by the window. The first mate watered them for him.

When I pulled in the smoke I felt a new warmth mix with the warmth from the rum, and then a coolness push the burning heat from my wounded shoulder and arse.

"Moon's Widow," Wallace said. "From Fracia. I met a doctor there, when I had occasional business with a gang known as the Grimers. He, too, had occasional business with them. Their leader was more beast than man, name of Butcher, nice teeth, but no skin on his face. None at all."

I tried to picture that as I handed the pipe back to him, but couldn't. He took a puff then returned it to me. By this point the mixture of the rum, the herb, and my injured, depleted state made everything seem hardly more than a dream. I felt free of repercussion and so I revealed things I had not spoken of, or even thought of, in years.

"I wanted to be an actor when I was a child, Wallace." I looked at the dead lizard on the stone floor. I put my hands out in front of me, then panned them slowly out to the sides and whispered, "I had dreams of the stage. And… and I fear I have been acting on the deck of this ship, acting a hard man." I paused and took another puff, and returned the pipe once more to that good man Wayward Wallace. "But I am afraid, not so much of dying, but dying in the fight that's coming. I'm scared of that. I hope a bullet gets me before the swords are loose. I really do. I have no wish to stare into the eyes of my killer."

"Agree. I would much rather stare into the eyes of those I kill," Wallace said. I turned to him and he was looking at me, and then he wrapped his arm round my shoulder. He was many years my elder, and had taken a liking to me since I joined the crew; he and the captain both had. I was lucky for that. "Just don't think much about it, Golden Boy," he said as he released his hold. "It's only death, and it's only killing. It's just part of the dream, you know?"

I did not weep, but my eyes went warm and my cheeks got wet. *Just a dream, free, like a dream.* The captain's words. Words she often used to remind us where she had come from, what she had achieved, what all of us could achieve if we only dared dream.

"I have to do this, don't I?" I asked Wallace.

The sounds of the men throughout the fort preparing for

CATACOMBS OF TIME

battle carried to us: the bark of the captain's orders, the scrape of heavy objects dragged across the floor, feet slapping stone. He took another long hit from his pipe, and he spoke as he exhaled so his voice became very deep.

"Yep, you have to. You're one of us, Golden Boy, you're one of us. Took me a while, too, to get in there, right into the whirlwind of blades. But I'll tell you what: it is quite a special thing." Wallace handed me the pipe, and I pulled until my lungs were on fire and held the smoke there in my chest, then I finally released. A purple haze veiled my vision.

Wallace stood, went to the firing hole, and looked out of it.

"So, are you ready, Golden Boy?" he asked with his back to me, then he turned and his eyes were wide and he was grinning ear to ear, his pigtails draped over his shoulders. "Are you ready to live the dream?" He threw a musket to me, and I caught it.

"I'm ready, Wallace."

He nodded, dipped his chin toward the dead lizard, and said, "They bite. The wound festers. And then you die. Did no one tell you that?" Without waiting for my answer, he continued, "Go on with you now. See you at the other end."

I set the musket beside the others and made my way back down the stairs. The captain's voice carried from below as she gathered the men.

I paused just inside the door of the gate room where the men were gathered, and the captain stood in the center, sword at her hip, her blue coat, a trophy she had stolen from one of the church's Seekers after she cut out his heart, nearly dragging on the floor, fury in her eyes.

"I remember my first time," she began. "Six months north of here on a fast ship, on the western coast of the new world continent where tribes of cannibals and Lycans stalk the shores searching for survivors from wrecked ships. The golden tails of sirens glinted beneath the water's surface. They would at times rise from the water to lure men to the rocks and into the cold abyss with their naked, milky flesh and sweet siren songs."

We could all hear the rumble of the purple coats' snare drums down the beach. But it was the captain who held our attention.

"The waters were calm and the wind was a cold breeze carrying drifting flakes of snow. That was my first time seeing snow. It was hypnotizing as it fell silently from a gray sky. I watched my breath melt the flecks in front of my face before they reached the deck. They just faded in the vapor that left me. And I remember marveling in my own mind that just six months prior in the waters round this very isle that we now hold, I was freed from a slave ship heading to Brynth by Filthy Jack Lawrence and the crew of the *Sea Maggot*. They slew every slaver to the last, and Captain Lawrence offered every woman and child on the ship a voyage to the next isle, where they would be left with coin from the dead slavers. And to every man he offered revenge.

"'Come with me now,' he said. 'Come with me on my journey, a journey toward bloody death, a journey free of shackles, a journey that will set the foundation for our sons and daughters to one day drag the kings and queens of the old world and the governors and ministers of the new to their own gallows and watch them dance as they are choked by their own ropes. It won't be us,' he said. 'No it won't be you or I who see that day, but come with me and let us make damn sure it will be our sons and daughters who see the thing done. Who see the dream.'

"I stood up. I was the only one to stand. Filthy Jack looked at me with his bloodshot yellow eyes and grinned his black, putrid smile. His lips curled and he took from his head his worn yellow tricorn, ran a ringed hand through his slimy hair, and said to me, 'That offer was for the men, so unless you're hiding something in your trousers, I don't think so.' Filthy Jack's men hollered with laughter.

"'You lost two men,' I said. 'Taking me on is better than none. These women and children are the wives, sons, and daughters of these men. They want a chance to live. They are in no rush to die. My family has already been taken from me.'

"'So you are in a rush to die?' asked Filthy Jack.

"'I'm in a rush to use this,' I said, and I pulled from my trousers a sharpened stake of wood, a stake I had plied from the wall of the hold where I'd been chained, my nails bleeding. A stake I had honed to a talon-sharp point by rubbing it against the chains that bound me. I raised it to Jack. And of course he smiled and laughed.

"'So you *were* hiding something in your trousers,' he said, and his men started laughing again. 'Well, it's a start, but I'm not sure if it will be quite enough.'

"'I've been swinging a hoe, a shovel, a rake, a pick for those pig-skinned men all my life,' I said to Filthy Jack. 'Give me a fucking sword and I'll show them I can swing that too.'

"'Young lady,' said he, 'you'll be mistress to death himself one day. I see it in your eyes.'

"'You're wrong,' I said.

"He cocked a brow.

"'I'll be his queen.'

"At this his rotten smile grew and he gave me my sword. For six months, as we went north to the cove that he and his crew called home, I was taught day in and day out, in sickness and in health, the blade and the gun. And then that day finally came, the day that I had been preparing for, the chance to fight the fiends who took me from my *home* and killed my parents in the garden outside of *theirs*. I was filled with fear. I was not afraid of dying, but I was afraid of dying before I ate my fill of revenge, and I was starving. My legs shook when I heard the Monkey cry, 'Sails,' from high in the rigging, and they shook all the more when I saw the Brynthian juggernaut's shadow emerge from the white curtain of falling snow.

"'Load the guns. We'll fire the forecannons as we charge them and give her a full broadside at point blank before we board.' Filthy Jack roared the order. We went forward, the wind with us. The Brynthian juggernaut was preparing to fire her full broadside at us. This was before we had Stiggis on our deck, and our wizard at the time was only any real good at card tricks and lighting things on fire, so their guns were a very real danger.

"I was standing next to Filthy Jack as we closed the distance. I had a saber at my hip and was clutching my pistol in my hand. 'When it comes to those things, don't blow your load early,' he said, pointing at my pistol. 'Use it when you're losing with the sword or if you're at a numerical disadvantage. No other time, and never rely on it as your only way out. Make them shoot first'—he grinned at me—'and always make sure they miss—'

"'And don't let their screams slow you down,' I finished for him. He chuckled and raised his looking glass, where he watched the shadow of the enemy captain through the snow on the deck of his ship, and when he saw the man's arm go up to give the order to prepare to fire their volley, Captain Lawrence gave our order. 'Fire.'

"The swivels and front cannons erupted and the *Sea Maggot*'s deck quaked beneath me. We hit them just before they released the wrath of their broadside upon us. It disrupted their aim and their shots went too high.

"'Pull your socks up,' screamed Jack, and I hit the deck as the hot iron balls whistled over my back, ripping through the rigging and taking off the rotten maiden's head, cutting slow men in half and reducing the captain's quarters to splinters.

"Filthy Jack sprang back to his feet and with the voice of a joyous man, he gave the order: 'Fire the swivels at will. They'll rake us with another volley before we have her in our claws!' I couldn't see what he saw. All I could see was death coming for us all in the form of a bigger ship, more guns, and more men. But I trusted the dream. I was ready to die for the dream, to die free rather than live shackled.

"I could smell the man's wicked breath from a meter away. His bloodshot eyes bulged as if they were about to burst, and he was smiling like a lunatic, red running down from his scalp, a splinter of wood pinning his tricorn to his head.

"'Oh, here it is, young lady. Here it is. I feel it taking me,' said Filthy Jack, and he grabbed me by my shoulders and shook me as the *Sea Maggot* closed the distance. 'After it begins you'll feel it too, young lady. If you're to be—' He turned and yelled, 'Pull your socks up!' and we hit the deck again. The *Sea Maggot*'s main mast was chopped in two and our sharpshooter Higgins screamed as he fell into the frigid blue. 'If you're to be death's queen, oh, you'll feel it,' Filthy Jack yelled to me as he sprang back to his feet and gave the order: 'Turn her broadside, ready to board!'

"Every man on deck, and I the only woman, we roared, and as I heard the sound of cries of hatred for the Empire, I felt it. I was wet for it. The bloodlust had taken me for the very first time."

When our captain reached this moment in the story, we hollered and whistled. That day with a few hundred of the Empire's men on our shore, with Admiral "Gallows" Gareth spearheading the assault, we roared our cries of hatred, for we felt it too. The bloodlust had come, healed our wounds, and made us strong. As we roared, the admiral fired his cannons at the fort, and for a moment the world shook and my heart pounded in my ears. And then we were cheering, for the fort held, and it would hold long enough for us to get to the end of the captain's story.

"The rotten maiden scraped across the Brynthian juggernaut's port side," she said as dust fell from the stone ceiling. "Our starboard flattened against them.

"'Fire!' ordered Filthy Jack, and the cannons that had kept their load for so long finally released, and we ripped that juggernaut's inside apart. The men gathered on our starboard side, muskets, pistols, sabers, and boarding axes in hand. Our wizard ignited many of the crew's drawn blades with fire, and we must have looked like demons straight from hell's pit. The Brynthians fired their volley of muskets and pistols first. Fear made their trigger fingers twitch. They fired without aiming and they fired too high.

"Filthy Jack wore two pistols at his hips and four on his chest, and he fired off all six with the devil's speed. Then the boarding planks were down. Our sabers were drawn. Men were firing pistols and muskets into the men on deck of the Brynthian ship.

"'With me!' cried Filthy Jack, and we crossed the threshold. My boots splashed into sleet from the snow mingling with the blood of the men shot dead. The snow was falling harder now, and it became near impossible to see ten feet. At his instruction, I stayed behind Filthy Jack, guarding his back as he hewed down men like a god of war in a celestial dream. His silhouette in the snow hacking apart the silhouettes of his foes, spraying red through the curtain of white."

Another cannon volley smashed into the fort, and this time it hit its mark. The front gates were reinforced with iron, but they were not invincible. They'd open soon, and four hundred purple coats would be charging up the narrow beach between the high stone walls that protected the wharf, a bottleneck that would work to our advantage, but for how long?

The captain strapped on her pistols, two at her hips and four on the torso. All of them had once belonged to Captain Filthy Jack Lawrence, as had the saber she wielded. We parted as she walked down the center of us. Her steel leg clinked on the stone floor.

"A purple coat slipped round Jack and, saber high, he swung down at me. I parried." The captain demonstrated, bringing up her blade in an arc with such speed that in the dim light of the fort the motion was invisible. "It was Jack's teachings, it was bloodlust, and it was my will to live that blocked that strike. I heard gunshot—"

As if on cue, another volley of cannon fire hit the gate, and splinters sprayed the interior as dust again fell from the ceiling.

"In the corner of my eye I watched the silhouette of Filthy Jack take sabers to his chest and belly. I watched him fall. I fought like a cornered hyena, and still I could not reach him, for the man I fought had size and strength and years of experience that I lacked." She paused and drew a breath. "Oh, how I screamed. Tears burned down my cheeks, the first tears I ever shed over a pig-skinned man. A great man. Wrongly, I thought him dead. The bloodlust peaked in me and I stuck my saber into that Brynthian bastard's belly. I twisted right, then left, then hauled up and split him to his breastbone. He was a tough man, and furious and frantic, and he did not die right away. He pulled himself further onto the blade, and I pressed into him and pulled it down, forcing him to his knees.

"I raised my pistol and stuffed it into the purple coat's screaming mouth, and with my saber in his belly I pulled the trigger, and out the back of his skull onto the sleet-covered deck went the man's blood, brains, and my hot lead. The snow kept falling and the fight kept thrashing around me.

"I remember him, that first man that I killed, but those

who came after are all a blurred memory of ecstasy and bliss, of melancholy and hate." The captain grinned and lifted her saber high. "I remember my first time."

"Now hear me, my truest friends. What makes us kin is not the tone of our flesh. I care not if you're as pale as a pig or as black as a boar. Or as golden and pretty as Golden Boy." The men laughed, and I laughed with them.

"We could have gone down at sea, for that would have been a glorious death. But we did not, though not without sacrifice." She paused, and we all thought of the men we had lost, and of Stiggis fighting to the end. Again came the roar of the cannons, shaking the world around us. "They think we are done. They think they have the wounded fox in a corner. And they do. But the fox is cunning, wily, and full of tricks." She paced as she spoke, meeting the eyes of the men she passed. "To finish the job, they will have to come into our corner, the one we call home. And in our home, in the dark and the wet, they will break, just as the crew of the *Tide Mauler* broke, and the crew of the *Lucky Rabbit* broke, and the crews of the Empire's best we slew on the beaches of Fracia last year broke. Facing the crew of the *Sea Maggot*, the most feared fucking crew on all the seas, facing them close as lovers, hacking them down in the shadows, they will break."

"Aye!" we roared in answer to her, for though there was no chance we could win, she had reminded us of the dream. We howled like animals, the animals they wanted us to be, the monsters in the cave that the heroes of the Empire came to slay. Yes, we would be those monsters, and they would feel our claws and teeth.

They were there now, right outside our doors.

"Pull your socks up!" cried our captain, and we all hit the floor as the gates came apart and fragments of iron sprayed into us.

We wheeled our three eight-pound cannons into the

breach and waited.

"Form line," ordered Admiral Gareth from behind the advancing rank of hundreds of men on his high fucking horse. "Fire!" he yelled.

"Fire!" roared our captain, and as she cried it out, in my fevered state her eyes were glowing red.

Our cannons released, sending an eight-pound sphere of iron to hit a purple coat square in the chest, bursting him into a mist of blood and chunks of meat. The shot did the same to the three men behind the first. When the cannons were fired, our pistols and muskets erupted and more purple coats went down. Wayward Wallace unleashed hell on them from the left tower with his Deck Sweeper and muskets and globes of fiery death. Rays of sunlight leaked in through the cracks in the primordial stone, and they illuminated the purple coats as their blood sprayed over the white sand of the beach.

One of our men pressed against my back, and my chest was shoved up against a purple coat whose allies were pressing him in the same manner. Close as lovers. I could see every grain of stubble on his jaw, count each eyelash, watch the sweat beading on his forehead. I gripped tight onto the man's musket with my left hand and tried to find room to stab his neck with my saber in my right hand, unsure if it was truly the crush that stopped me, or something else entirely. We were at an impasse, until the captain killed the man she was facing, drew one of her pistols, and deafened me as she pressed the barrel to the skull of the man next to me and took his head off.

The press of bodies around me eased. I was loose for a moment, the space to stab out given. I committed. I took it. I recall every feature of the man's face and I remember the sound he made as I plunged my blade into his lungs. I felt no shame, no repulsion.

It had finally taken me—on the island of Poino, on the precipice that marked the boundary between stone and beach, the bloodlust truly took me for the first time. I pulled my blade free and danced with my captain as she barreled forward on her peg leg, firing her pistols and hacking men down. I danced at her back. We danced together, the green boys and the veterans alike, to the sounds of screaming and grunting, muzzles booming, blades clashing. We followed death's rhythm, and before night fell we turned the Empire from our wharf, from our cave, from our fort.

We showed them that they were not the only ones who could reach out and take at will, that beaten dogs are dangerous when they form a pack and are raised by a wolf.

A decade has passed since the battle at Poino. I now stand on deck as Captain Timothy "Golden Boy" O'Connor of the *Sea Maggot*. Your captain. Before us is an armada of fifteen ships flying the black, a wizard on every deck and an army of beaten dogs looking to sink their teeth into the throats of the men who showed them the boot heel. Look there, lads, to the fleet of Brynth guarding the shoreline, with Admiral "Gallows" Gareth at its head, he who fled my captain and her crew all those years ago. I will kill that man, but before I do, I tell you of the glory, the brutality, the beauty of the bloodlust.

I tell you how I remember my first time.

End

Grab the next book in the series—The Pyres—now!

Join Dylan's reader group for the latest news about contests, releases and more!

ALSO BY DYLAN DOOSE

SWORD AND SORCERY SERIES:

Fire and Sword (Volume 1)

Catacombs of Time (Volume 2)

I Remember My First Time (A Sword and Sorcery short story; can be read at any point in the series)

The Pyres (Volume 3)

Ice and Stone (Volume 4)

As They Burn (Volume 5)

Black Sun Moon (Volume 6)

Embers on the Wind (Volume 7)

RED HARVEST SERIES:

Crow Mountain (Volume 1)

∼

For info, excerpts, contests and more, join Dylan's Reader Group!

Website: www.DylanDooseAuthor.com

ABOUT THE AUTHOR

Dylan Doose is the author of the ongoing Dark Fantasy saga, *Sword & Sorcery*.

Dylan also pens the new Dark Fantasy/Western Horror series, *Red Harvest*.

Fire and Sword was chosen as a Shelf Unbound Notable 100 for 2015 and received an honorable mention from Library Journal.

For info, excerpts, contests and more, join Dylan's Reader Group! www.DylanDooseAuthor.com

photo credit: Shanon Fujioka

For more information:
www.dylandooseauthor.com